STOLEN BRIDE

STOLEN HEARTS

CARINA BLAKE

THE STEELE PRESS

No one crosses me unless they wish to meet their maker.

My past made me the devil I am today, but in walks my angel, trying to break that mold against my will. She is innocent and broken, engaged to another, but she doesn't belong in my world. Still, I won't let her walk away without giving in to the long-awaited desire I've denied myself, even if it is temporary. Once I've taken care of our enemies, she can leave with tarnished feathers, blackened by my need. Then, I'll let my angel fly away — if I can.

PROLOGUE

DAMIANO

The kill felt good, and now I'm hard as stone. My hand strokes my cock. Damn, I never knew how much pleasure I'd get out of taking down so many pieces of shit at once, but I was too damn good at it. The blood washes off my body as I work my shaft.

Maybe I'll take my grandfather's offer and finally take a whore, but my father wants me to wait until I have a little more control of my emotions before I start fucking my way through the city. Maybe he has a point, but my grandfather does too. At sixteen, I've already killed ten men. Why is sex a big deal? I need to nut, and my hand is getting stale.

Still, it'll do the job right now. "Fuck, yes," I groan, nutting quickly. Damn. Maybe my father is right. I need more time to get my hormones in order because that was almost faster than pulling the trigger. I wash off my mess and then scrub my body clean before turning off the scalding hot shower. Stepping out into the steamy bathroom, I wrap a towel around my waist and then wipe my hand across the mirror. From my face and physique, I'm one sexy bastard, looking like the damn devil in the making.

Lifting my watch off the counter, I have an hour until I meet with my grandfather to go over tonight's business, so I better get dressed because he prefers that I'm dressed impeccably. We share an intense bond, he and I, and I've learned so much from him, including his sense of style, and his thirst for blood.

When I step out of my bathroom while drying my hair with a towel, I see a pair of bare legs dangling off my bed that are far from hairy, and all feminine. Lifting my gaze, I find my grandfather's new wife, Sarah, a plain name that is the complete opposite of her personality. She's the love of his life, thirty years his junior, and she is sitting naked on my bed with her legs open, looking like a forbidden meal waiting for me. Instead of being tempted, I feel a rage that I never felt before. "What the fuck are you doing in here?" I bark out. I turn around instantly.

"Don't do that, Damiano, baby." I thought having a beautiful, naked woman in my bed would be the biggest turn on in my life—and from the state of my towel, it would seem so—but it's not what she thinks.

"Don't fucking call me that. Get your clothes and get the hell out of my room now before I do something we both regret."

She stands up, and I think she's going to leave, but her hand touches my cock. "Oh, I don't think you'll regret it." She has no idea how wrong she is. Bloodlust gets me hard, and I want her head for her treachery. I didn't like the woman from the moment I met her. I pull away, sending my towel to the floor. I'm about to reach for the blade in my drawer when the door opens and in walks my grandfather.

"How the fuck could you?" he roars, his voice so fueled with deadly anger and pain. I think he's talking to her, but when I look at him, the bastard is actually staring at me. My hero, my nanno, is staring at me like I'm the sick, disgusting predator—the cheater.

"It's not..." I don't get to react before he pulls his gun on me. The shot is taken, hitting me in the chest, but I'm quick and I reach for my blade, sending it flying into his gut. "You fool," I groan, shaking my head as I fall to the ground.

"That was easier than I expected," she says as she leans over me, laughing evilly, turning my now cold heart to stone.

The sound of feet come running. "Papa! Damiano!" my father roars.

"Get that bitch," I groan. I hear a loud crack before the lights go out and she screams.

"Tie that bitch up. My son needs a medic." My father takes control, but through his strength is his fear for me. He holds a towel to my chest, pressing his forehead to mine. "Rimanere forte, mi figlio."

Those are the last words I hear for a month. From then on, I am a changed man. No longer the dark, young mafia boy in training, but a young man with an icy heart and an itch to kill anyone who puts their hands on me. With my father's strength, I remained strong and held on, but now the love I had was just for three people, my mother, father, and baby sister. Everyone else could rot in hell, and every bitch could fuck off. I'd never let a whore come near me, touch me, breathe near my dick again.

CHAPTER ONE

DAMIANO

Grace dances in the middle of the floor with fuckers eyeing her young, feminine figure as she shakes it, and I want to line them up and run my blade across their necks as I rush by in a furious rage, but I hold it together because she's trying to have a good time.

Grace is nineteen and celebrating her birthday with a night out with her only friend. After having a late start, she was forced to finish high school a year later than most, so she's letting loose tonight.

The Miami heat can be unforgiving, but tonight is a cool night. The club is packed with bodies heating the room, even with the air turned to a cool sixty-five. I run one of the most expensive and classiest dance clubs in the city that caters to the young and wealthy. Still, I don't trust the rich fucks wanting my little sister in her skimpy outfit.

My eyes scan the room, and I don't spot the little harlot. I had instantly taken a disliking to her friend, Camille Jones, from the second she stepped in my way. She screamed opportunist a million miles away with her snake eyes leering at me, but I wasn't an easy mark for a little girl like that. So, with a warning glare, I sent the little girl running. Still, I didn't want the girl loose in my club doing the hell knows what.

I walk up to my muscle, Adriano, and ask, "Have you seen the little tramp that came in with my sister?"

"Last I saw her, Rocco was escorting Ms. Jones to the restroom." Oh, that's good, because my men know the rules and would keep her well behaved. I gaze toward the restrooms on the other end and see the line is long. My brows knit together, and I turn to Adriano for answers. "That was about ten minutes ago, and the line is getting long."

"What the fuck?" We have more than enough stalls for the ladies. It was a big thing to ensure we didn't have long damn lines, so what is going on? Normally I'd leave that shit to someone else, but my gut tells me this has something to do with Grace's friend.

I'm walking toward the door when I hear a woman say with a mouth full of disgust, "Damn. I didn't realize they allowed that in the club."

I confront the woman, who flinches and then stares at me with intrigue, as most women do. "Excuse me. What is allowed in the club?"

"There's someone getting…" She shakes her fist back

and forth from her mouth, mimicking a blow job. *Motherfucker.*

"Thank you. Excuse me. One minute." I rush past all the ladies.

"Any time, handsome. If you want the same…" I feel the air shift as she reaches for me, but I'm already out of reach. Still, I have a point to make, fixing the clear misunderstanding about the behavior permitted in my establishment.

I turn back and glare. "You do that in my club, and you'll be out on your ass." The realization of who they just met washes over their overly painted faces, and it pleases me. Fear sets in, and they step back.

Now, back to the mission at hand. I slam the door open to find Rocco spraying Camille in the face in the middle of the ladies' room. Somehow, I expected no less.

"Get the fuck up off your knees and wash up. You will not be going anywhere with my sister." I address my piece-of-shit employee next. "Rocco, you're lucky I don't put a bullet in your head. Get the fuck out of my face." They're both quick to straighten themselves up from a sight I didn't need to see.

"Sorry, Boss. It's just…" My fist lands on his face before he gets to finish whatever he has to say.

"What part of 'get the fuck out of my face' didn't you understand?" As the boss, I don't repeat commands, and the bastard made two mistakes tonight.

I storm up to my office to wash my hands and check for any blood. Luckily I'm clean because I'd have to give Rocco an extra couple gut checks for it otherwise.

Digging out my cell from my inner suit jacket pocket, I

call Gabriele, my underboss, because I have to cut Gracie's party short. Despite the noise in the club, he's quick to pick up. "Yeah, Boss."

"I need you to escort my sister home, and don't let her give you any shit. I have matters to deal with here tonight, and she brought trouble to my club."

"Will do. What about her friend?" he asks.

My blood boils, remembering what I witnessed. She doesn't need to be sending my sister down that slutty path. "No, that slut can call herself an Uber or pay someone else with a blow job for a ride."

"Yes, Dame." Gabriele doesn't have to ask questions and handles matters swiftly. My father doesn't trust many men to guard my sister, but in addition to Adriano, my underboss is one of the few allowed to guard her, but I need him for my business tonight.

"Don't let me down. I need to have a talk with Rocco when the club closes, so get her home safely and return quickly."

"Understood." I end the call as I see my guest arrive. The pudgy bastard is already sweating, and it has nothing to do with the hot bodies grinding in the club below. He pulls out his handkerchief and swipes it across his sweaty brow with his meaty hand.

My security leads him to my office and knocks on my door just as I move to sit behind my desk. "Enter."

"Thanks for seeing me, Mr. Valentino." His platitudes aren't needed. Business is business, and the sooner I get him out of my sight, the better.

"What is it that you believe I can do for you?" I

question, regretting this meeting as he sweats profusely in front of me.

"I need a temporary loan." That's what we had previously discussed when he requested an audience. He turns his attention to my wet bar, eyeing the booze nervously. Yes, I intimidate people, but Tommy Baker isn't usually intimidated by others. He's not a mobster like me, but his hands are nearly as filthy as the men he works with. He could never catch up to my darkness, but I'm interested in why he looks petrified.

"Yes, I am aware of that, but how much and for what extended period of time?" He's wasting my time by having to pull it word by word from him.

"Please explain why I should hand over $100k to a man I don't know."

"I'm a very talented businessman, Mr. Valentino."

"Obviously not that talented as you're here looking for a handout, sweating like a pig and looking awfully nervous. Why would that be?" I lean forward, staring into his cowardly soul.

"I heard of your reputation, is all," he stammers.

With a nonchalant raise of my brow, I ask, "And the loan?"

"It's a temporary situation, and the banks are not that interested in lending to a strip club owner."

"Understood." I sit back, watching him ease up. "What kind of collateral do you have to offer me, Tommy boy?"

"I could pay you back within a month."

"So you say, but that doesn't mean anything to me. You're just a man looking for a handout, Tommy. What have you got that makes this worth my time or my money? I don't hand out loans to just anyone."

"I'll put up my company."

"You mean your strip club?"

"No, I mean my investment firm."

"So you have two businesses, and you can't afford your own debts."

"I can't embezzle funds to pay off the debt of the other, Mr. Valentino."

"I don't want the investment firm. It's too much work to see its value, but a strip club could be an easy business. However, I'll only take the club if I don't get my money within the allotted time."

"Understood."

"We'll make it thirty-five days?" I offer, knowing his original suggestion was stupid and short-sighted.

"Yes, that's more than I need." He waves his hands manically.

Scoffing, I raise my hand to stop his sputtering. "You say that now, but I don't want you coming back pleading for more time because I'm not the forgiving type, Tommy."

"Yes, Mr. Valentino. Thank you." I stand up and walk to the wall safe in my office that's hidden behind paneling, and I open it while I use the bathroom mirror to watch Tommy's greedy eyes on me. He has no idea that's the reason the door is still open—or that I don't normally carry funds in there on days I don't have reason to—but I want to see what this weasel's on about.

Handing over the funds, I state, "Now—let's shake on the deal, and you can be on your way. I'm quite busy."

"Yes, Mr. Valentino. Thank you, Mr. Valentino." Many would be pleased with his sycophant behavior, but I find it suspicious, although I don't let on and send the sloppy bastard on his way. I head to the bathroom immediately to wash his stink off my hands.

"Rocco, what the fuck am I going to do with you?" I ask of one of my favorite soldiers. He's been with me for four years, and I'd hate to have to drill a bullet in his ass. "Give me one good reason, Rocco."

"Boss, I didn't mean to do it. She was hot, and she slipped me a pill when she kissed me. Before I knew it, I was feeling really fucking good…too good." If she gave him something, it could explain why he would break my club rules for a quick release when he could easily have taken her out to his vehicle.

Fisting his hair, I drag his head back and stare into his beady eyes. "You wouldn't be lying to me, would you?" I ask, reading him.

"No, I swear, Boss. You can test me. I swear it's still in my blood."

"Call the doc," I tell Gabriele. "If you're lying, I'll chop your balls off. You weren't supposed to kiss the teenager in the first place, but there are better places to blow your load than in my club and ruining my reputation." My place has class for a reason. It keeps the cops from digging into it and my other assets, and it's the way I'd prefer to maintain it.

"She caught me off guard." There's no doubt about it.

Camille has a practiced way about her. Foolishly, she tried to use it on me, and I immediately shunned her advances. If that bitch tried to slip some drugs to me, I would have slit her fucking throat.

"That's because you're weak and you're just interested in chasing pussy all night. You're on my shit list. Any more fuckups, and it will be the last thing you do. Understood, Rocco?"

"Yes, Boss." He bows profusely, thanking his lucky stars that I didn't just whip out my gun and put a bullet in his head for defying my orders. The doctor arrives within ten minutes.

I stand up and round my desk to shake his hand. "It's good of you to come so quickly."

He looks exhausted, which means he probably had been on call when I summoned him. "I was at the scene of an OD at the strip club down the road." I was right. Another reason I don't want drugs and sex in my club. "What can I do for you?"

I point to the jackass sitting on my sofa. "Rocco believes he was given some sort of drug that made him horny enough to violate my club's policy. I want to know if he's lying. He said it was slipped onto his tongue."

"I'll take blood and urine samples as well as a cheek swab." Nodding, I wave him off and let the doc do his work while I move back to my chair and go over this evening's numbers. Once the doctor's done, I thank him and send both of them on their way, but not before paying the good doctor for his expedited services.

Once they are gone, I pour Gabriele and myself a drink. Handing one over to him, I take a seat on the edge of my desk and ask, "How did my sister take her dismissal?"

He takes a long pull of his whiskey before twirling the tumbler in his hand. With a sigh, he answers, "As you'd expect. First, I was blamed, and then she complained that you ruined her night."

Just as I expected. My sister is a lot like my mother, but sometimes I see my father in her. "I'll tell my father to make it up to her, although I would like to have a talk with Grace tomorrow before work. Let's head out of here before I find someone's head to smash in today."

He rolls his head and cracks his neck, tension vibrating off him. "Sounds good to me. There were several guys you could have lined up after the way they were eye fucking little Gracie."

"Don't remind me." We leave in the early morning hours, and I head over to my parents' estate because I want to speak with my sister when she wakes, so it's best that I just stay the night. My head hits the pillow in my old bedroom where I easily pass out for my normal five hours.

I'm at my parents' home waiting for my sister to speak to me, but she's staring at her food like she's ready to kill her bacon all over again. "It's already dead."

"Pity. Just like my dating life. Don't you have someone else's life to ruin?"

"Not yet. Not until I straighten some shit out with you."

"There's nothing to straighten out. You told me that I

could come to your club and you wouldn't ruin my night, but you did anyway. I could have gone anywhere else and had a great time for my birthday."

"Look at me, Hummingbird. I didn't fuck up your night. Your little slut friend did that."

"What does this have to do with Camille? Just because she hit on you? Come on—like women don't try to hit on you."

"It wasn't that. I caught her in the bathroom with one of the guys, violating my club rules."

"What?"

"Yes. I was livid. People were talking about how the club operates."

"So why did I have to go?"

"Everyone saw you together. If anyone said a damn thing about you, I would have slit throats that night."

"Maybe I should stay away from your club."

"You know damn well Dad will not allow you to go anywhere else. I just don't want that whore with you."

"Understood."

"I'm sorry, Hummingbird. Don't take it out on Gabe. He was just protecting you."

"Protecting me? He was snarling at every single man that approached me."

"Exactly. You have no idea how many times I considered killing all of them last night. You're my baby sister, and those perverts only want you for one thing."

"Because I'm only worth that?"

"No, but they don't know you. All they see is a beautiful woman who was half-naked and shaking her ass all over."

"You have problems." She rolls her eyes.

"And?"

"How do you think people meet?"

"I don't know. I have no intention of having a wife or a family, so it doesn't matter to me."

"Again, Dame, you have problems."

"I love my life, Hummingbird. I just want someone who is worthy of you, but you're not going to find that hanging around with trash like Camille Jones."

"Fine, but she's not that easy to shake," Grace says, taking a drink of her orange juice.

"I could take care of her." It's an offer that I wouldn't normally make when it comes to a female, but this one is already proving to be trouble within my club and with my family.

"No. She might be promiscuous, but that doesn't mean she deserves to be buried." I suppose I may be overreacting, but I have my standards.

"Whatever. Anyone who crosses me deserves to be buried."

"Problems." She shakes her head and finally bites into her bacon, but not before I snatch another piece. "Now that's a capital offense." Smirking at her, I wink and walk away while shaking my head.

CHAPTER TWO

STELLA

The sunshine burns violently through my window like a damn death ray. "Shit," I grumble. Normally mornings bother me, but not this much. After a long night of suffering with a wild headache and an evening of cleaning the entire house, my head and body are exhausted. Not to mention the start of the Miami heat has kicked in. We are about to be bugs under a magnifying glass on a hot day for the foreseeable future.

I crawl out of bed and dress for the day before my verbal alarm clock goes off. My life sucks, and it's only a matter of moments before my day is about to get worse. I slip on my shoes and then brush my hair. I'm about to tie it up when I hear the pounding hooves at the foot of the stairs.

"Stella, get your lazy ass out of bed and down these stairs before I drag you down here," my stepfather bellows.

"Coming," I called out with the hair tie in my mouth. Rushing downstairs, I hurry into the kitchen where my stepfather is already eating his breakfast bagel and drinking his coffee. "Prepare my eggs and don't make me wait any longer. There's much to discuss today."

I make quick work of his breakfast and work on my oatmeal. Although he has something to say he doesn't mention it throughout the entire meal. In fact, he intentionally dismisses any attempt at conversation and focuses on his tablet where he has his morning stock reports.

When he finishes his eggs and bacon, I pick up the dishes from the kitchen table and move toward the sink. "Please join us for dinner tonight, Stella," my stepfather says. I freeze mid-step with the plates in my hand. My fingers shake violently, and I nearly send the ceramic dishes cascading to the floor, but despite my flood of fear, I know better and set them on the counter next to the sink.

"Is there a reason?" I choke out, fighting my terror.

He slams his chair back, and it skids across the wooden floor, hitting the wall. I try not to react, but my brain is hard-wired to flinch. "Because I fucking said so, Stella. You will do as you're told."

"I...I...I only wondered if it's a special occasion. Something I should wear?" I answer, hating how petrified I am and wishing I had the nerve to stand up to him.

He takes a calming breath. "You need to learn to speak properly. Your best clothes."

I swallow hard, trying to control the vomit in my throat because I had a feeling this day would come. A girl like me doesn't have many options in life, and it's clear those choices are being taken away from me. I nod and turn around to wash the dishes, hiding the tears that ache to fall from my eyes. Whatever tonight holds, it will be the end of any real future.

"Don't act like a petulant brat. I've given you a better life than you would have had if I'd sent you to a home." He mutters something under his breath that I can't hear, but the last bit I do. "Nice piece of ass." My breakfast threatens to come up, and I pray he wasn't referring to me.

Still, I finish the dishes before he has a reason to come into the room and punish me. When I'm done, I head into my room and dig through my outfits, but I have nothing nice. The man hasn't bought me a pretty dress in five years, and my body has grown out of most of the clothes. Luckily, everything I'd gotten before had been bulky because I've matured and my figure fills in the rest.

The door opens without a knock. "Holy shit," I screech out, pressing the small dress to my chest, barely covering my breasts.

"Relax. It's only me." Camille rolls her eyes like it's not a big deal to have someone just storm into your room when you're half naked. She's carrying an armful of dress bags. "I figured you didn't have shit to wear. So, I picked up some new outfits." She tosses them on the bed and then turns to the open door. "Close the door, Tony." Oh my goodness. I can't believe her. "Daddy said he wanted you to appear hot, so these will have to do. Not that you'll look better than me." She giggles as she finishes her words, giving me a cursory glance.

When she utters those words, I understand what tonight is about. I'm meeting the man my stepfather wants me to marry, and that means I will be marrying him if the man finds me appealing. "Shit."

"Girl, get that out now because you know Dad isn't going to tolerate your attitude and mouth. This is for the best, and you know it." He's my warden, but she's just another one of the guards. Camille has never been anything more than a cruel stepsister.

Although she's like her father, she's never hit me, so I don't mind speaking up with her. "The best would be me getting a job and maybe a college education. Finding a husband by choice."

She waves off my concern. "Come on—this guy is wealthy."

"So you know who it is?" I ask, hoping she'll give me some details.

"Um, not really, but I know my dad." My stomach drops because that means there's a financial deal in place. That's the only reason he's eager to spend money on clothes for me.

"So, what do you think I should wear? We're not even the same size." Even though I want nothing to do with this, getting new clothes would be nice.

"I know. I'm about two inches shorter than you, so these dresses are going to show more ass and tits." *Damn it.*

She pulls out the tightest and most revealing dresses. "If you knew I was taller and everything, why didn't you just get a bigger size?"

"Me going into the store and asking for a larger size? Ugh." She presses her hand to her chest as if I insulted her.

There is no doubt that I'm screwed. I pick the least offensive dress in the pile.

"Of course you'd pick the safe one. It doesn't matter. I'll keep the rest and maybe let you borrow one if he wants you for a second date."

"If he wants me, he wants me, so there's no need to show him every inch. What's the phrase?"

She cuts me off. "Yeah, yeah. He'll pay for it all." So she knows that the bastard is willing to pay for me. I bet her father wouldn't sell her off to anyone, but since I'm his stepdaughter, I'm fair game.

It's time for dinner, and our guest is about to arrive. All afternoon, I thought about his looks, his age, and his attitude. If he wants me for marriage, then he has to be a total loser.

"Where is Camille?"

"She won't be joining us tonight. She has better things to do. This is just for you, so you better make it worth my effort." My body is full of nerves as I await my fate in the living room. The doorbell rings, and my father goes straight to the door.

"Welcome. Please come in, Thomas."

"Good evening, James." I hear the greeting, and immediately the voice tells me he's not young, as if I had any hope to begin with. They sound similar to each other. When he enters the room, I have to hold back my revulsion at the large, balding man in his late forties.

His eyes rake up and down my body, tracing my figure

like a sick vulture. "She's gorgeous, Jimmy." He licks his lips. "You weren't lying."

I gag. "Excuse me."

There's no way I can marry that man. No way.

I run from the room and vomit as soon as I make it into the bathroom. My stepfather comes bursting into the room, fisting my hair, gripping it violently with evil eyes that shake me to the core. That hasn't happened since I was a little girl. With a deadly expression in his eyes, he whispers through clenched teeth, "Wash your mouth, get your ass out there, and behave. You'll pay for this outburst later."

He releases me hard, and my hands barely catch myself against the sink. A moment later, I've managed to compose myself and then exit the bathroom, moving to the dining room where they're gathered. As soon as my presence is known they're attention is on me and I can't help but feel like a spotlight is on me. Still, I give him my fake apology as demanded. "Sorry. My breakfast hasn't sat well with me."

He gives me a snide look and then smiles. "It's okay. I'll make sure it's taken off the menu." Every urge I have to vomit is held back as I politely return his smile.

"How old are you, Stella?" I'm sure he's already aware, but he wants to hear it from my lips.

The bile fills my throat, but I manage to swallow it back. "I'll be eighteen in a few weeks."

"Good. Good." There's a sinister appearance on his face as he focuses on my mouth. "There's so much I can do with that pretty mouth of yours once you're legal."

"The wedding should take place right after her birthday," my stepfather says.

I drop my fork, but I haven't forgotten the warning I'd gotten. "Behave, little girl," Thomas says, taking no issue with correcting me in front of my stepfather.

"Don't worry. She'll be disciplined for her behavior."

He smirks and takes a drink of his wine. "Remember— I want her to be perfect coming to me, so no damage to her face and that innocent little hole."

"Of course." The smirk on his dirty face was something I haven't witnessed before. I bite my tongue because they both just agreed that my stepfather could abuse me as long as he didn't hurt my face or fuck me. I've never been more disgusted.

I just want the night to end. Mercifully, I'm sent to my room before Thomas leaves, but that doesn't stop the punishment. It's in the middle of my sleep when I'm awakened to being pulled from my bed, the belt landing on my body several times. He grips my bicep violently and forces me to stare at him. "You ever disrespect and embarrass me again, and your marriage to Thomas won't save you from what I have planned."

He tosses me onto the floor, and the pain radiates before I black out.

CHAPTER THREE

DAMIANO

As the party gets underway downstairs, my night is only beginning. Bodies dance on the floor below while the music thumps and the drinks flow throughout the club. Given my reputation, it's a money-maker with little to no trouble because no one is stupid enough to come in here and start problems—a reputation that is well deserved.

Technically, the club is a legal establishment, but that doesn't mean my actions aren't well known. I am dangerous, deadly, and take shit from no one. It's the reason my club is called *Body Count*. It's not the number of women to fuck, because that's the furthest thing from my mind. No—my bloodlust drives me in life, pushing me forward daily.

I may be considered the most ruthless mob boss in town. Still, the authorities mind their fucking business. Paying to have the right people in your pocket is instrumental in life. A lot of those pieces of dirt are so corrupt that they almost make me appear clean. Although, nothing could do that. I'm sick, deadly, insane. My soul is colored blood red, and my heart is darker than night.

My underboss sits across from me as we review last night's figures. "It's prosperous, as usual."

"Yes, it is," I mutter, looking at the raw sales. We're making a killing every night, but something is nagging at me. Although I can't put my finger on it, I feel it down in my marrow. It might have to do with one of my other assets because the club doesn't seem to be the issue.

Lately, there has been a lot of chatter about another family wanting to move in on my territory and practically begging for a war. It's a fight I'll gladly give them while their blood drips off my smiling face.

After twenty minutes of perusing the numbers, I close the ledger before me and glance up at my underboss with the slightest upturn of my lips. The numbers in the club for the quarter look great, which pleases me. There isn't much that satisfies me, but the success of my empire is one. Someone's head on my chopping block is my next favorite pastime.

"Something bothering you?" Gabriele asks, reading me well. We're the only two in my office. My muscle, Adriano, guards the door to prevent anyone from interrupting us while Rocco handles the prep for opening the club. Rocco's on my shit list for getting a blow job from my sister's friend in my fucking club. He knew damn well that it was against the rules for the patrons. He was lucky the test had proven he'd been drugged.

Besides the fact that I couldn't stand the slut from the

second she entered my club, something about her sends an unease through me. Her motives are too devious. I wonder if she's still trying to burrow in close with Grace.

"You're lucky you know me so damn well, or I'd think I was giving myself away," I chuckle, ready to toss my pen at his head.

He smirks and adjusts his suit jacket before dropping a bombshell. "Could it be that Baker didn't invite you to his wedding?"

I sit up straight, eyebrows raising. Did I hear him correctly? "Let me get this straight. Tommy Baker is getting married?" My head twists to the side as I stare at my longtime friend and underboss. "The Tommy Baker that owes me a fuck-ton of money?" I repeat. I can't believe what I'm hearing. Running my fingers through my smooth, thick black hair, I'm shocked. No one wants to marry that fat slob, so that woman has to be getting paid big time.

He nods, sitting back in his chair. "That's the piece of shit. I learned of it this afternoon. I'm not sure who the hell Baker had to bribe for that task, but he's going to get hitched to some young woman in a couple of days or something. His bachelor party is at Scarlett's tonight."

Scarlett's is a strip club owned by Baker. It's a run-down crack den these days with hookers for strippers who give you more than a dance. Their dirty snatches pass you a disease on the way out. I almost feel bad for the dumb broad he managed to trap. *Almost.*

"I can't imagine getting tied to a woman." My face scrunches up, while Gabe smirks. I shake that thought out of my head with a bit of panic. Even though he's my bestfriend, I never shared my past with him, including the fact that I actually despise whores and innocent girls are rare and too good for the devil like me.

My parents are happily married, but I have no intention of putting a woman through that hell. My heart is too damn dark for that shit, especially for someone as soft as my sister or mother, who are the epitomes of sensitive and sweet. My father married a woman who was his polar opposite, and my sister is a replica of her. They are good in every way, making being mean to their sweet faces hard. Although, I will do what I must when necessary, which makes having a wife more trouble than it's worth—so much trouble that it would affect my work.

In fact, my father is so obsessed with my mother that he turned over the reins of the empire to me when I was twenty-three because he wanted to devote time to her. It didn't help that I already had a ruthless appetite, yet he still gave up everything to worship her, something I couldn't do for anyone.

The devil in me was born and bred from day one, which my father believes I got from my grandfather, who was a total bastard. Not complaining, because at one time he'd been my hero who taught me to be ruthless, but then he was my biggest enemy. He is the reason I'm the man I've become, if I can even be called a man. He taught me to be ruthless and unforgiving; the final lesson culminating when I took his life for his betrayal.

Most consider me a monster in a suit—a well-tailored suit. I'm not meant to be a husband or a father. No, I am Satan in the flesh. I enjoy ripping people's souls from their bodies for the slightest offense.

"I can't see you married either, but who would you leave your empire to?" he asks. It's the million-dollar question that my father has asked me on many occasions. He knows what I did, why I don't want a connection to anyone. I've ruled with a bloodlust since I was sixteen and haven't looked back.

"When my sister finds a husband and has kids, they will inherit it." There's a slight tic in his jaw and I wonder what that's about, but I don't have time to question him on it because we have more important matters to handle.

He rolls his wrist around to check his watch. "It's almost time for our meeting," he says.

Smirking, I think about the next order of business. The darkness that lives within me seeps out, stretching across my face with pride. "Yes. Salazar should be arriving for our private meeting."

"Do you believe we'll need a cleanup?" Gabriele asks me, looking over at my new wood floors. I had them installed to withstand heavy spills. They're easy to clean; still, we don't want a mess.

"I would prefer to have an amicable result to this evening, but you know that may not be possible." I do my best to maintain a straight face and test him.

"You'd prefer?" He tilts his head like he doesn't believe me. The fact that he can read me is starting to get fucking annoying.

I toss my hands out and say, "Okay, fair enough, old friend. I want his head on a spike, but I'd also like my money and not have a problem with the rest of his family." They're on the verge of becoming a pain in my ass. A pain I didn't need, but I never pass up a good fight.

"It's not like we can't take them all out simultaneously, but it's not impossible." Engaging in a big blood bath would be a bit sticky, and there would be the risk of others taking their place.

"True. Are you getting as bloodthirsty as I am?" I question, smirking.

"Don't give me too much credit. I just don't like the guy." I wonder why that is, but it's not the time to ask. Lately, he's been acting differently. I have a feeling there's a specific reason—or rather, a person—but it's a personal matter. We have to be ready for our guest and postpone the necessary discussion.

"Fair." I stand up and tuck the ledger away in my secondary safe, locking it up just as there's a knock at the door.

"Enter."

"Boss, we got Salazar outside," Adriano says, standing in the doorway. That motherfucker is massive and takes up the entire space. I don't know what his mama was feeding him, but I'm betting it wasn't just the fucking milk from the cows, but the entire cow since he cut his first tooth.

"Have him brought in quietly in two minutes." He nods and then exits quietly, closing the door.

I shake my head with a smirk. "Damn. It still amazes me how someone so large can move so silently." Neither Gabe nor I are small by any means, but Adriano is a tank.

"Glad he's on our side," he says.

"That's for sure. Let's get this shit over with." I take a seat behind my desk while Gabriele grabs a plastic wrap from a locked cabinet and sets it under the rug so Gus isn't spooked by its presence. Can't get what I want if he sees his death imminent. I will have to replace my nice area rug. At least I ordered several over the years for just such an event.

A knock at the door brings my nervous guest. "Hello, Gustavo. Take a seat." I glance at the bloodied lip and busted eye and know he chose to put up a fight. It might have been the smart thing to do because he's more than likely not walking out of here.

"No, I'll stand." The defiance rankles me, but I don't show it.

"I'm sure that wasn't a fucking request." He sits quickly. Gabriele stands behind him while Adriano and Vito wait by the door just in case he decides to get bold. No one is getting past them, so I'm more than at ease.

"So, we have a problem. I've been waiting a long time, Salazar. Where is my money?" It's the determining factor of whether he lives or dies tonight.

"I paid you." I chuckle, and so does Gabe because he's sealed his fate. Salazar gets more and more nervous, body rocking side to side in the chair.

I lean forward in my seat, pressing my hands firmly on my desk before I ask, "Really? In what? Imaginary funds? Monopoly money?"

"No. Maybe your guys didn't give it to you." He tilts his head, tweaking. We should have seen it sooner.

"Are you calling one of my men a thief? Be careful on that because if I have to call them on it, I'll be making sure that everyone pays double for the deceit." I stare at him, knowing he's bullshitting me. The motherfucker doesn't have two nickels to rub together. He's gotten hooked on his own supply.

"Okay, okay. I don't have it."

"So here is what's going to happen. You're going to turn over all your property to me, and I'll let you walk out of here." It's a generous offer. One that I wouldn't make to most people, but he does have some decent properties that I could use to my advantage. Besides, I'm positive he's not going to take my offer.

He tries to jump out of his chair as he protests. "Wait. Hell, no." Gabriele grabs his head and slams it back, putting a knife to his throat.

"I wasn't finished." I step around my desk and sit on the edge, directly in front of the filth who thought he could scam me. "I've given you more than enough time to pay me, so that's the deal. Take it or leave it."

"I'd rather die than give up my property." Why are these guys always so damn full of brass balls, as if I'm going to somehow back down?

"Deal," I say.

Gabriele steps back and pulls the rug as I shoot the fucker between the eyes. "Stupid bastard," Gabriele chuckles, shaking his head as Gustavo's lifeless body falls onto the plastic, limiting the mess in my office.

"He should have taken my deal." Looking at the clean rug makes me smile. "Thanks for saving the rug. I liked that one."

"Me too."

CHAPTER FOUR

STELLA

"You're getting married in two days. You need to live a little before you're tied to that slob for the rest of your life." I shiver in disgust while she continues to pester me by tugging on my slender and already bruised arm. "Come on. It's not like we can't get past your nannies on duty. They're puppets," my stepsister Camille says. For her they are easily manipulated, but they watch me like vultures on an easy meal.

My stepsister and I hate each other, and yet, this is something I can't disagree with. Since I was ten and my mother married her father, I was never once allowed any freedom or fun. When I was younger, friends were limited to the girls at my school, and boys weren't even an option.

Now that I've turned eighteen, I'm being forced to marry a man that nauseates me at the mere sight of him. Hell, just hearing his name makes my stomach roll. The first time I saw him, I nearly vomited on his shoes. I excused myself and ran to the bathroom, blaming it on my breakfast even though my stepfather didn't believe me. Of course, I was later punished with a severe beating.

"You know you want to go clubbing tonight, girl," my stepsister's best friend adds, brushing her long blonde hair in my room. They've been in my room since this morning, bugging me. I actually like Gracie, and I'm not actually sure why she's friends with Camille because they're nothing alike. She's totally perfect, beautiful, smart, and her hair shines like a diamond. The only blight on her record is her friendship with my evil stepsister.

"I don't know," I say, feeling unsure about this. Camille's a total cunt and we don't get along one bit, but a taste of fun for even just one night sounds great—even if I'll pay for it later. I'll be spending the rest of my life submitting to a piece-of-shit loser who works for the mob or something like that. One night of fun sounds wonderful. My fiancé is supposed to be someone important, but I met the man. He comes in with his shirts rumbled, clothes less than neat, and gross looking—a total slob.

"You do. Have a little fun before you have to deep throat Tommy's sausage roll." I swallow the bile that instantly fills my mouth. Damn it, Camille is such a bitch.

"Ew. Must you be a disgusting bitch?" Gracie says. Even she has the decency not to remind me how horrible my future will be. The internal anguish building every hour feels unbearable, and I can't tell if my evil stepsister is truly unaware how awful this is for me, or if she honestly relishes the torture. It's more than likely the latter.

"I'm just saying it's what he's going to want." Death is looking better and better every day, but I don't want to give them the satisfaction. Still, I'm not sure I can stomach being married to a filthy monster even for just a minute.

"Yes, and now I'll be a vegetarian for life." Gracie gags, pressing her hand against her mouth.

"Girl. Please, just come out tonight. It will be your bachelorette party. He's having his stag party. The guards are minimal. You get one last final hurrah, and it'll be a blast." Camille gives me a pleading stare.

"Fine." I relent and cave to their pleading.

"Yay!" they squeal like preteen girls.

"And you can't back out. We're going to my bedroom to find some outfits for tonight." She points her finger at me, and I give her a silent nod, hoping she'll give me some peace. Thankfully, she does, leading Gracie to the door.

The girls leave me in my room alone. I have no interest in what they pick because I want to dance and drink to forget what's going to happen. Maybe I'll even get my first kiss by a man of my choice. A man who doesn't make me sick to stare at. Someone who stirs a hint of interest. It doesn't even need to be insane lust or love at first sight because I don't have time for that, but I want a shot at something of my choosing—just once.

Closing my eyes, I allow myself for the first time a fantasy of meeting a tall, dark, mysterious stranger while the music is so loud we can't hear more than the pounding of our own hearts. Will he cup my face, look deep into my eyes, and command me to give him my lips?

It's too much, and I feel the pleasure down to my core

as I imagine his lips falling on mine as I let out a moan. My hands grip the worn-out pillow and bring it to my face, only to have my bedroom door fly open.

"Girl, we were calling your name for like two minutes," Gracie says.

"Trying to suffocate yourself?" Camille adds. "It's not going to work like that, dummy. Anyway, get up. We're getting ready to leave."

"Ugh, whatever. How are you going to get me out? You know I can't leave."

"Don't worry about that."

Twenty minutes later, we're packed up and ready to leave the house with the extra clothes in our overnight bags. All we need to do is talk to her father about the sleepover at Gracie's.

My stepsister is allowed to leave without asking for permission, but she needs to get approval to take me with her. I stand at the bottom of the stairs and listen to their conversation. He's sitting on his favorite recliner watching the Heat game. When he sees Camille, he pauses it. "What's going on, princess?"

"Hey, Dad. Stella and I are going to Gracie's for a sleepover."

"Have fun." He waves. My hand clasps over my mouth with shock because he didn't stop me from going.

"Wait." I think he's going to tell her, "Hell, no," but then he asks, "Is her brother going to be around?"

"I doubt it. He doesn't live there." I'm not sure who her brother is or anything, but he's supposed to be popular and wealthy. Camille hasn't even formally introduced me to her friend because I'm not important enough, so I don't know her as anything more than Gracie.

"Pity. He's rich, and you could try to meet him." Of course he wants to push a hot guy who isn't old or gross toward her.

She waves off the idea like it's stupid. "Anyway, I was thinking of doing a makeover for Stella before the wedding. One nice little sisterly bonding thing."

"That's so sweet of you, pumpkin." I want to roll my eyes, but it's actually what we're doing so I'm looking forward to having my hair and makeup done.

"I know, right? She should be grateful, but I'm sure she'll find something to complain about. Anyway, we'll be leaving soon." There is the Camille I know.

He looks at me and glares. "You better behave, young lady. Don't think you're going to be plotting any escape while at Miss Grace's. Tommy's guards won't be far from the house," he warns me with a sneering wag of his finger.

"I know. I'm not going anywhere. I know I'm a prisoner for the rest of my life," I mutter that last bit, but his eyes bulge out, having heard every word.

"Don't act like a little bitch. You've been given every privilege when you came from nothing. Your mother was a dirty whore, and now you're getting a chance to marry up." He loves to degrade her even though he's the one who visited her workplace weekly, paying for sex because he couldn't get it for free.

I fight the anger building up in me because it's only going to get me hit again. I've already gotten a bruise from this morning's outburst. My future husband-to-be doesn't care that my stepfather hits me as long as I have all my teeth and he doesn't leave any scars. So, bruises are more than okay if I deserve them, which they both agree I do.

Sometimes, I feel like the only way out is the ultimate way out. I've considered it more times than I should. Maybe it would be better to find help, but who can I trust? Everyone seems to be on his side, and the only time I was able to confide in a teacher, I was pulled from the school and transferred to a special school where I was no longer allowed to have private discussions with teachers, and friends were out of the question.

"Yes, Stepfather." I nod and walk away. He's quickly on his feet and grips my forearm, spinning me around.

"Did I dismiss you?" I mask the pain and shake my head. "Answer me, little bitch."

"No, Stepfather."

"That's right." He wrenches my arm downward, releasing it violently, sending pain through my shoulder. I yelp, but I don't shed a tear because I can't let him see me cry. I learned a long time ago that he enjoys it too much, and I'm done giving him the pleasure.

"We've got to get going. Gracie's parents are pretty strict about people coming to their house after eight," Camille says, defusing the situation.

"Okay. Run along and have fun." I follow my stepsister and Gracie out of the house with our bags.

Gracie gives me a stare of sympathy, but Camille rolls her eyes and says, "She knows her place, and yet she does things to get herself in trouble." She always acts like I deserve it, too.

I don't say a word because all I want is to go out and get wasted, forget about what my life will be.

"So, how are we getting out of your house?" I ask Gracie as she drives us away from my stepfather's home.

"My parents aren't home. They're in Bali on their second honeymoon. Tonight we're going to my brother's club, and he'll let me in because I'll behave, but that means we'll be closely watched by his men." She gives my stepsister a warning glance, and I wonder if there's going to be a problem.

"He's not going to rat us out, will he?" I ask, hoping that we don't get caught.

She scoffs. "My brother doesn't snitch. Although, he might send us home if we get out of hand, so we have to at least behave, which means no fucking guys in the bathroom, Camille."

I pretend that I'm not shocked about that little bit of information. I had no idea that my stepsister was having sex with men let alone in bathrooms. "It was one time. Geez, I don't know why your brother doesn't like me."

"He has rules, that's all." As we drive on, a realization strikes me. She's not doing this for me at all. Camille can't get into the club without a good reason after burning her bridge with Gracie's brother, and now I'm the reason. We get to Gracie's house, and she leads us up to her bedroom. "Leave everything here and change. I'll do your makeup soon. Just let me change." Within two hours, we're ready to leave.

"Okay, we're going to be on our best behavior," she says, giving Camille a warning. She looks at me and whispers, "You can have fun." She tosses me a wink before sliding into the back of the car with her driver taking the lead.

Anxiety fills me as we get closer to the club. I have never been out of the house other than to school and back in so many years, and definitely not to have fun. I've defied so many rules tonight that I know I'm gonna be punished heavily, and yet the excitement inside me grows.

The second we pull up to *Body Count*, the driver opens the door for us. Gracie exits first, followed by Camille, while I step out last, tugging at the hem of my short dress. Gracie grabs my hand and leads us to the front of the line. The security guard outside the club recognizes Gracie and smiles. "He's not gonna be happy that you're here… with her." His gaze lands on my stepsister. But then his eyes fall to me and he adds, "But who the hell are you?"

His stare lingers too long, enjoying every inch of my figure, and that annoys Camille. "She's engaged, jerk."

"I don't see a ring." He pointedly glances at my bare fingers.

"That's because she's out to have one last night of fun. Keep trouble away," Gracie warns him with a tip of her chin and an arch of brow.

He scoffs and glares right at Camille. Damn, she must have a really shitty reputation here. "You brought trouble with you. You're lucky you are the boss's sister."

He lets us through, smiling at me one more time. I nervously enter the club and am bombarded with loud music that drowns out all thoughts.

Camille drags me straight to the bar, which isn't legal, but she's obviously not one to follow rules.

"Oh, no. Boss told me you were off limits, girl." The woman looks at me and says, "Never seen you before."

Her earpiece blinks and then she steps back, holding up a finger for us to give her a moment.

"Ugh, seriously. I need a drink," Camille complains.

Immediately a man slides in between us, facing me. "Hey, beautiful. I'll buy you whatever you want."

"Okay," she answers.

His eyes land on me, lingering longer and more lecherously than the doorman. "I was talking to your friend." I'm not interested, but I am thirsty.

"If you buy her one, I need one too," Camille says, pouting at him.

"Sure. Anything for a pretty face." He hasn't taken his eyes off me. Another bartender appears, and he gets us a drink quickly. The guy takes it and then slides it into my hand. "Here you go, sexy. You need to loosen up."

I'm not sure I can do it, but Camille tells me to relax and hands me hers, telling me it's sweeter. "Hold your nose and drink it down in one gulp." I do, and although it tastes a bit funky, it's not terrible. This will be my only time getting wasted, so I might as well enjoy it.

"Wow, sweetheart. Slow down or I'll be carrying you over my shoulder tonight," he whispers against my ear. His hot breath turns my stomach, and I want to shove him away.

Suddenly we're crowded by a hulking man who I have to crane my neck back to look up at and has to be almost as wide as I am tall. He looks down at us and says, "Boss wants you two up in VIP now."

"The ladies are with me," says the guy who bought our drinks, sliding his arm around my waist.

"Get the fuck lost, or should I tell Mr. Valentino we have a problem, Ernesto?" the beefy man snarls.

"No problem, Rocco." He throws his hands up. "See you around, beautiful." He winks at me, grabbing my ass, and I gasp, wanting to swat his hand away, but Rocco pushes him first.

"That wasn't wise, Ernesto." The threat in Rocco's voice reminds me of my stepfather's men.

"Just showing my girl a good time." I don't even know this dude, and I'm not interested in the least. Why is it that the first guy to hit on me is a sleazeball?

"Where's Gracie?" I ask, trying to defuse the situation. Besides, we lost Gracie the second we came into the club. Since she's the owner's sister, I'm sure she's safe, but I'm still curious.

"She's already up there," he grumbles.

"VIP?" Camille asks, looking annoyed as hell.

"Yes," Rocco answers.

"He's trying to keep an eye on us. Let's bounce," Camille tosses out, tugging me.

"I don't think that would be wise, little trouble," he growls, giving her a look that instantly gets her to behave. He leads us upstairs to a private lounge before calling the server, who brings us some drinks. Rocco slides closer to me with his large thighs touching mine, giving me an unsettling feeling. I think the alcohol is getting to me, and my head is spinning along with the club lights.

Then, out of nowhere, the air in the lavish space changes. I glance up and see a tall man in an all-black suit. He's not nearly as broad as the brute next to us, but there's a natural danger to his presence. His stare meets mine with his dark gray eyes that are almost the color of steel, and a deep shiver washes over me. I know that I've become his prey.

Immediately I duck my head as my heart slams against my ribs. There's nowhere to run as he stands at the only exit. I'm at his mercy, and for some reason, I know he's not one to grant it.

CHAPTER FIVE

DAMIANO

They say I'm fucking crazy, and they may be right, but he has it coming. "Clean up this mess," I order my men, pointing to the dead body on my office floor. The bastard shouldn't have crossed me and then dared me. It's like begging for a hole in the head. He's lucky I didn't drag out his death, which I regret now since it went too quickly.

I step into my bathroom, quickly cleaning myself up. Fuck, I got some blood on my suit. It's why I always wear black. It makes the stains a little less noticeable.

My phone hasn't stopped ringing in my pocket, which pisses me off. It's my security at the front door, so I know it must be important enough to interrupt me. "Boss, your sister's here tonight." A rush of violence fills me up. Someone's going to end up killed tonight. Well, someone else.

Son of a bitch. I ought to ban her ass, but then she'd sneak off to another club.

Grace tried that shit once, and luckily Gabriele caught her before she made it there or I'd have had to hunt her down and kill a bunch of other fuckers who couldn't keep their hands to themselves. She's too young to be in any club, grinding up on men with nothing but screwing on their minds.

I'm not one to mess with, and my sister is off-limits to everyone. I'll rip a bastard's balls off and feed them to him before I gut the fucker and show them to him one last time as he dies. Last month already tried my patience, and now she's here again.

"I want eyes on her," I warn him.

"She's not alone." The words come out of his mouth with a nervous stammer because *don't kill the messenger* is a warning I need often. My blood boils instantly because I'm not aware of any friends other than that one bitch I told her to stay away from.

Taking a calming breath, I say, "Please tell me it's not that dumb bitch." It's suddenly like everyone wants to defy me. That shit isn't going to fly.

"It is, but she's got someone else too."

"It better not be some man." My sister wouldn't be foolish enough to bring some asshole here to die a painful death because that's exactly what would happen. She's only nineteen, and although she hangs out with a little whore, she's a good girl. They met at school, and my sister thought she could be an excellent influence on her. I warned her about hanging out with that lousy cunt. It's something we're going to discuss very soon.

"No, it's another chick, but this one is hot as hell and damn, a bit shy, but she's here apparently having a bachelorette party." What the hell is an eighteen-year-old doing having a bachelorette party unless her friend has an older friend or relative?

"Thanks. I'll deal with them," I tell him because I want this shit cleared up and the trouble sent home immediately.

I radio my security, Rocco, on the floor and have him bring the girls to my lounge area. Normally I'd host clients there on occasion, but tonight was private business that got a little ugly. There was no way I could host anyone up here without the risk of them seeing or hearing anything messy.

There's a knock at my door, and Gabriele goes to check it. "It's Gracie." Damn. She didn't hesitate to get an earful.

I glimpse over to the now empty spot where Salazar had once laid, and even the bloodstain has now been picked up. "Let her in," I grunt, annoyed to no end at this moment with my little hummingbird.

"Thanks, brute," she says, slapping him in the chest. He grunts like it actually hurt, knowing it wasn't more than a fly swat on a horse's ass.

She goes up to hug me like she always does and stops in her tracks. Her brow arches, and a smirk spreads across her face before she steps away. "Getting sloppy, Brother." She reaches onto my desk, pulls out a tissue, and returns to my side, wiping my face. "Missed a spot."

I step back and stare at my baby sister with a look of disappointment to see the damn scandalous outfit she's decided to sport tonight, like she's asking for me to snap some necks. This club has maintained a clean public record, at least so it would seem. No bad press has been mentioned, but I've had to take people out that put their hands on her.

I snatch the tissue from her and tuck it in my pocket. "Thanks, Hummingbird. Now that you've interrupted me while I'm working and brought trash into my club again, what am I going to do with you?"

She twists her lips with a pleading look on her face. It's the same one she gives my father that has him bending at her will. It works for both her and my mother, but I'm not as easily amenable. "Listen, I swear it's out of the kindness of my heart." She does have the soul of a saint, even though she has gotten used to my business, but some people aren't worthy of her tender heart.

"That bitch doesn't deserve your kindness." My voice is cold and unrelenting, sending my sister a step back. My teeth grind so hard they're bound to crack with the anger I feel toward her friend. It isn't that I find her to be slutty. That's nothing. It's her attitude in general that sours me. Reading people is something that comes natural to someone in my world, and her friend has got "treacherous bitch" written on her forehead.

"Don't be mean, Damiano." Grace rolls her eyes at me, which I try to ignore, but my temper's growing and I'll take it out on my men later. "It's not for her. It's for her stepsister. She's a doll. I wish she had a different family, poor girl. Trust me when I tell you they are night and day."

Shaking my head, I walk into my private bathroom and look in the mirror to check my appearance once more for any stains. "Don't be fooled, my little naïve Gracie."

She follows behind me, standing against the doorframe, and tries to argue. "I'm not *that* naïve."

My brows shoot up and I lift my head away from the mirror, turning my attention back to my little sister. I give her a chance to explain what the fuck that's supposed to mean. She's a five-foot nothing with dark curls and doe eyes, looking ever the little girl I've always thought of, but there is something that makes her appear older. I don't like it. "Anyway, do tell me why you risked my wrath by bringing them into my club."

She rolls her eyes and gives me huff. "Stella is being married off in two days."

I tilt my head in confusion at the choice of words. An odd way of saying getting married. "Married off? Like an arranged marriage or some shit?" I ask.

"Yes, and she's obviously distraught about it. They're so cruel to her. Like, seriously, her mother died a long time ago, and they treat her terribly. I saw her stepfather hurt her, so when Camille used the excuse of taking her out for a last hurrah before she marries, I thought it would be nice to sneak her out to have some fun. I don't think she knows what fun is." She chokes on the last bit, tears filling her throat.

I walk up to my sister and swipe the tears off her face. "Don't cry, Hummingbird. You're too damn soft for this world." I'm going to kill the stepfather of this unknown girl for making my sister cry. She's used to my cruelty to men who deserve it, but I'd never harm a woman, even that friend of hers, unless she did something to Gracie. This bastard upset my sister so much she's shaking.

She swipes at her cheek with the back of her hand as

the tears continue to fall. "I'm sorry, Damiano. I swear, I hate her father. He was so mean. I used cover-up on the bruises, but they're still visible…a little."

"Bruises?" I ask, feeling my temper amplified for this unknown woman. Strange—normally, I wouldn't give two fucks. Perhaps it's because she's friends with my little sister.

"Yes. She has several." I thought I was pissed for my sister, but my anger's building for this young woman. No man should put his hands on a woman unless it's for pleasure.

"If it will make you happy, I will join you all for the night." It isn't just to make her happy. Protecting Gracie is always a priority, and I'm not going to let some girls take advantage of her. At least, that's what I tell myself. No one else matters to me except my family, so I shouldn't care about this woman.

"Thank you." She hugs me tight, something only she's ever been allowed to do. I don't let anyone touch me. Not a soul is deemed worthy of getting close to me. Her friend dared to get close, and my guards quickly pulled her back. It was another strike against her in my book.

"Come, now, before your friend gets her stepsister into trouble." I led my sister out of my office, through the catwalk, and over to my personal lounge.

Sitting there is Camille with Rocco, and meekly beside him is pure heaven with a drink in her hand. Long brown hair in waves is locked up in a tight ponytail, needing my fist to pull her head up and give me her attention. As if she senses the silent threat pouring out of me, she lifts her eyes to meet mine, and the cold, dark bastard in my soul has grown darker. They're a light blue that shine in the darkened club light.

Filthy thoughts shoot through my mind a mile a second as her lips part. *Yes, you've met trouble, little girl.* I envision sliding my ten-inch cock deep between those plump beauties and watch as she chokes on my dick. What the hell? I immediately harden against my Canali slacks, grateful that my tailor took good care in hiding my weapons. The enclosed lounge is good for business, and now it's going to be even more useful as she screams my name and looks down at the faces while they can't see a strip of her naked flesh. My balls ache to bend her over the lounge, screwing her while the crowd below dances, unaware that I'm filling her tiny hole with every ounce of my devil seed.

I want her.

I need her.

She's the devil's prize.

She is an angel with temptation written all over her, made for the devil. My heart fucking stops. There are only a few people this motherfucker beat for, and they are all family, but damn, it seems she just made that short list and moved to the very top. *What the hell just happened to me?*

This feeling makes no damn sense, and I want time alone with her to figure out what this temptress has used on me. Is it the bloody violence mixed with my anger just sending my adrenaline pumping that makes her more appealing? I will find out and squash these emotions before I let myself get out of hand.

"Rocco, get the fuck out of here. Take Camille dancing or wherever she wants to go. Get her some drinks as well."

I look directly at Camille with a look that should scare her shitless, but I wonder if she's too dumb or naïve to take me seriously. Instead, she stares at me with a look of indifference. "You, don't go whoring around my club."

"Yes, Mr. Valentino." It's good she doesn't have that flirty bravado she normally does. She learned her lesson the last time I warned her for even putting her hand on my arm, like she had the right. She's lucky I didn't rip it right out of the socket.

Still, none of that matters because all my attention is on the little thing in the black skintight dress that cuts at the top of her thighs, nearly showing her pussy from my angle. Fuck me. I'm going to cut some eyeballs out tonight. The number of men who have had a nice view of my future wife's cunt is unacceptable.

My shy little angel sees them rise and move to the stairs. Nervously she looks to their backs and decides to get up, thinking she's allowed to leave, but I never gave her permission to leave me. Shaking my head, I grip her hand in mine and sit her ass back down before taking a seat next to her.

Looking at my server who is waiting for us, I ask, "Bring us some bottles of water, please." I take my little woman's glass from her and set it on the tray. "She no longer needs this."

"Yes, Mr. Valentino." She leaves us, passing by my sister who has yet to take a seat.

"Grace."

Gracie looks at me strangely, giving me a smile before she says, "I have to use the ladies' room."

"My office," I inform her, returning my attention to my angel.

"Of course, Damiano." I can see my sister rolling her eyes without even looking at her.

We sit there all alone, and my body burns with hunger, yet my little angel refuses to give me her eyes. They remain trained to the hem of her short dress. Although it's a spot I find appealing as well, I want them on me. "Look at me," I command.

She lifts them in a flash, as though she's used to following orders. The first thing I spot is how glazed they already are. She's fucking already been drinking more than that glass, or she's on something. As pissed as I should be about that, I plan to use it to my advantage. My angel's engaged to another man, something I can't and won't tolerate. "Tell me your name, Angel."

"Stella."

"Stella, I'm Damiano." I take her hand and bring it to my lips, stealing a kiss on the back of her soft skin while noticing something so glaringly missing.

I rub her bare finger where her massive rock should be. "I thought you were engaged. Or was that an excuse to get my sister to bring you here?" I question, hating to think they lied to my sister and used her good nature to get inside my club, and yet at the same time, the pleasure of her being unattached is immeasurable.

"I am engaged," she hisses back in disgust, pulling her hand away from mine. Never in my life has someone dared to disrespect me without recourse, but there is something about her that makes my dick harder than it's ever been.

*Fight me—I'll enjoy the chase. I'll eat it up before I eat
you up.*

Still, I can't tolerate that she believes she belongs to
another man, or that there's some prick out there who
thinks he has some claim to her. The thought of him
putting his hands on her, touching her, kissing her, fucking
her, does violent things to my insides. A rumbling sound
builds in my chest as I rage internally, ready to shoot the
prick in the head.

Gripping my hand around her throat, I give it a gentle
squeeze. "Then where is the ring, because there's no way
in hell I would let my woman walk around dressed like sin
with eyes of an angel, *unclaimed*?" I lean in and brush my
nose over her hair, breathing her in. She smells so damn
good. I want to lick her from head to toe and mark her up
so every man knows she belongs to Satan himself. Even in
the darkness of the club lights, I can see her pale skin
redden at my compliment.

With her expression schooled, she says, "It's being
resized."

Smirking, I lean in, my thumb rubbing her chin.
"You're a good liar. A really damn good liar. But I'm
really good at reading people, baby girl. Now tell me the
truth. Those who lie to me find it's the last thing they do."
I wouldn't harm her at all, but I need her to tell me
everything. Her pulse picks up under my hand, and I
love it.

Something in my soul demands I act on her behalf. I'm
not sure what it is. Maybe that she's so sweet looking with
a hint of fire hidden under that demure façade or
something else, but my need to protect her grows stronger

with every second that passes. She closes her eyes as if she's absorbing my touch. As much as I don't mind, I want those beautiful blue irises on me.

"Answer me, Stella." My thumb caresses her cheek, sending her eyes back up to mine.

"I'm only allowed to wear it for show." Her confession is low and honest. I release my hold on her.

"Well, you're out tonight. Why aren't you wearing it?" I have a million questions. Some I'm too afraid of asking because it will send me into a violent rage, and no one will survive my wrath. The trail of dead bodies will lie at my woman's feet by the time I'm done.

"If they knew I was out tonight, I'd be a dead woman."

My knuckles whiten as I flex my fists, ready to do battle. I'll beat a motherfucker to death with my bare hands and not think twice about it. "They put their hands on you again, and I'll kill them."

She smirks as if she thinks I'm kidding.

"Sir." There's a light tap on the half wall. It's the server. I wave her in, and she sets the bottles down on the table in front of us. "Anything else?"

"No, thank you, Sasha." I might be an asshole, but my employees don't get treated poorly. She nods and steps away, leaving Stella to me again.

I pop open her water while I sit closer to her. As much as I want her to submit to me, and her being intoxicated helps, I don't want her to be trashed. My attention is captivated as she takes a sip of water, envious of the bottle against her soft red lips. Those plump beauties would be perfect wrapped around my cock, sliding over my length until she gags and begs to swallow my load. I bite back a groan as she sets the bottle onto the table.

"I'm serious, Stella. I'll end them all."

"I'm getting married in two days, Mr. Valentino." There's a sadness in her voice that destroys something in me.

I tip her chin up and meet her gaze. "It's Damiano. Say it."

"Damiano."

Gently shaking my head, I lick my lips as I stare at her mouth, aching to taste hers. "It even sounds sexy off your lips."

"Can I please have something other than water?" Her tongue pops out of her mouth, and I know she's itching for some excuse to let go of the barriers, an excuse to be bad. She doesn't need one. I'm all hers, and she's mine.

"Why?" I challenge her, brushing my thumb across her plump lips.

"I want to live a little before I..." Exactly what I thought.

"Before what?" She's going to say the words that will anger me.

"Before I get married." The words piss me off, like I expected. She's not marrying that asshole. I'm going to kill him either way, but every time she mentions it, I add another layer of torture to his death. If anyone mentions it, for that matter.

I brush her hair behind the shell of her ear, grazing my lips against her neck as I say, "Are you looking for liquid courage, my angel?"

"Yes," she answers shakily. Her body trembles in my

hold.

I pull back and look into her eyes. "I don't think you need it."

"I want it." Her voice is barely above a whisper, confidence absent.

"What did your sister give you before you got here?"

"Nothing. A guy at the bar bought us a drink, and then we got some when we arrived up here."

"A guy at the bar?" I want his balls ripped off. "Who?" I stand up and walk to the edge of the VIP barrier and look out toward the club as if I'm going to find this asshole. Rocco. He'd know. He grabbed them and brought them up here. He's got a thing for Camille.

"I don't know. We only just got here, and he said I was pretty and…"

"Pretty is an understatement, but it wasn't his right or privilege to do so, but what was the 'and'…."

"Nothing."

"Don't 'nothing' me. Tell me."

"Well, he claimed I was his girl, and he touched me before your guard snapped on him." Good. I'm glad my guard did his job, but he should have stopped him from touching her.

"He's a dead man." That's without a doubt. I'll destroy the handsy prick for putting his hands on my woman.

"I don't belong to you," she snaps. She's adorable when she's feisty.

"You're only lying to yourself, baby girl."

"Anyone can buy me a drink, you know." There's that liquid courage. Let's see how long it lasts.

"How old are you?" I press my hand to her mouth.

"Lie to me again and I'll take you over my knee, lift up your dress, and spank that ass."

She clenches her thighs together, like she's not opposed to the idea and she's trying to keep her pussy juices from soaking my leather. Fucking hell. My dick only stiffens harder. "I'm eighteen."

"You're not even supposed to be in my club," I inform her sexy ass because it's more than against the law. She's asking for trouble from all these sick bastards who want their hands on my woman.

"Well, neither should Gracie nor Camille."

I'd love to fuck away that attitude of hers until she understands who she's dealing with. I grip her chin with a little force. "Gracie's my sister, and if I never see your stepsister ever again, that would be a blessing. Now, tell me again that anyone can buy you a drink."

"Well, if I was old enough…" she pouts. It's fucking cute.

"No. They. Can't." I punctuate each word, tapping my finger on her nose. "Tonight, little angel, you made the mistake of coming into my club."

"I didn't make a mistake, Damiano. I came to have fun and be free one time before I'm trapped again and forever. If you're not going to let me have some fun, then maybe I did. We can always go to another club." She goes to stand, and that's when I've had enough. I thought I could be gentle and soft because it's clear she's a beaten animal who needs to be coaxed out, but that alcohol is taking effect and she's getting her courage. There is no way in fucking hell I'm letting Stella leave to meet with some other man wanting to do dirty things to her.

I grab her wrist and pull her onto my lap so she's straddling my thighs with her back to me. She yelps, and I remember what Gracie said. "Shit. Let me see." Lifting her arm, I inspect it to find the telltale fingerprints. Rage pumps through my veins, and I know that he'll never lay a hand on her again. I press my lips to the bruising and kiss it. "Sorry, baby girl. Sorry." I kiss them again. "Sorry." My mouth moves up her arm to her shoulder. "How much fun do you want to have tonight?"

"I have to be a virgin for my husband." I'm a devious son of a bitch because I don't care that she's on something: booze or drugs. She's wasted, and I'm taking what I need from her, making her mine, marking my territory.

"You're not marrying him," I growl against her throat, sliding my nose up her jaw and enjoying the way her pulse amps up.

"I'm getting married in two days." I crack my neck to the side until it pops and then let out a harsh breath.

With ice running in my veins, I ask, "Do you doubt me, Stella?" My hand snakes around her throat, caressing her smooth skin. Stella's pulse picks up, voice shaking as she tries to answer, but the words don't come out. My angel only nods. "You won't be marrying him. You belong to me."

"I can't belong to you." I turn her face with my thumb and then plant my lips on hers, silencing her denial because I don't want to hear that shit anymore. The more she says it the angrier I get, and that's not something she needs to see. My own anger doesn't make sense, and I don't want to assess that right now. What I want is her surrender.

CHAPTER SIX

STELLA

The heat from his breath against my cheek sends delightful chills coursing down my body. I want to give in to anything he demands, surrendering to all temptation. "Tell me you're mine." His deep, commanding voice almost has me giving in, but I can't because whatever this is, it won't last, and it won't change my future. I can't be his even if I want to.

Damiano is a nightclub owner with one thing on his mind, and that's getting me in his arms—and I need that too. His hand cups the back of my head, caressing me so tenderly that I fight off the moan caught in my throat and find my voice.

"I'm not yours. I'm getting married in two days." My words hit him like a slap in the face, and he's clearly pissed. Although I'm not afraid of him like I am of my stepfather or even of Tommy, I still don't want to upset this handsome stranger. I want to belong to him in ways neither of us can comprehend. We've only just met, and he's better than the devils I already know because his touch, his gaze, draws me in.

He chuckles. "You're cute. I almost believe that you believe what you're saying."

"I do," I huff weakly, trying to push off him. My body shifts just enough to rub my ass on his lap, grinding his thick length on my bottom, widening my eyes at the surprise. He's massive everywhere.

"Stella, don't lie to either of us because it's not going to do us any good. You're wasting your precious evening out, denying what we both want." He brushes his nose up and down my throat. "Tell me you don't want me to please you."

"I…I…"

My skin burns as his fingers trail down my arms, caressing my flesh.

"I want you to please me, but only for tonight." His room darkens and his eyes brighten, and I'm terrified of how much I want him. We are polar opposites in all ways, from his dark features to his devilish charms and expensive everything. I am nothing in comparison and yet, I can't deny the attraction.

"Surrender to the devil, little angel," he commands ever so subtly, and I do.

"Yes," I breathe out, parting my lips as he trails his mouth along my throat.

CHAPTER SEVEN

DAMIANO

Instead, I'll give her what we both want. "Open up for me." She parts her thighs. "Such a good girl, learning just what I want." My hand slides between her slender legs, stroking her thigh gently, working higher slowly to not scare her. She may be intoxicated, but she's too innocent for the deviant bastard inside me. She's so tiny that I slide her forward and lift her dress to reveal her panties. Fuck, the innocent white pair are soaked, hardening my dick to the point of pain. I'd kill to be inside of her right now.

"Damiano," she whimpers, pressing her hands on the leather seat, gripping the material.

"Tell me what you need, my angel. I want to hear you tell me how much I can take because if I have my way, I'll take it all." There's no way I give a fuck about this other asshole who thinks she belongs to him.

"Touch me." Her thighs open wider for me, but I need more.

"Give me your mouth." She dips her head and I kiss the soul out of her, sliding my tongue inside like I want to do to her tight wet hole. Her hands move to my biceps, nails digging, and I flip her so she's straddling me.

My hand slips under her dress, pushing her panties to the side while my thick fingers rub her pussy lips. "I'm about to fuck this tight little pussy. Tell me to stop."

"Stop, but I don't want you to stop." The yearning in her voice is in conflict with her attempts to push me back. The shove is weak as she grinds her hips forward and my one hand holds her firmly in place.

"That's because you're mine, and you know it." We both know the truth. I'm wrong for her, but my dick says otherwise.

"I can't be yours." I'm going to stop that argument now, even though she's right. She can't be mine because this little thing can't belong to someone as dark as me, but for now, I need this moment to be ours.

"Too late. You already are." I push my finger deep inside, claiming her pussy, and she cries out, coming on my finger while riding my ridge fast as fuck. Her moans are captured by my mouth, which is good because a sudden wave of possessiveness falls over me. There are way too many men who could hear her cries. The sound of an angel whimpering as she loses her wings isn't meant for the world. It belongs to the devil.

I pull out of her slit and lick the sticky mess of her orgasm and the pink tinge of the blood from the nick of her innocence, sucking the taste off my digit. I relish with satisfaction that she's mine. She belongs to Damiano Valentino.

Her eyes widen with shock, and then a sense of fear takes over like she's realized what she's done. Nothing she's done is wrong, because she's mine and no one is going to take her from me.

"I need to go." She jumps up just as I get a call on my phone. She gets off my lap and runs down the stairs into the crowd of people. My sister decides to make her reappearance.

"Get your friend back, and watch after Stella. Keep her protected at all costs," I growl, standing and bringing my phone to my ear.

"Yes," she says with a smile, dashing down the stairs after my future bride. There's no way I'll let someone steal Damiano Valentino's property.

"What the fuck is so important?" I bark into the phone.

"Someone has blown up the warehouse on Seventh," Georgio answers.

"I'm on my way." I end the call and run straight into Gabriele. "Someone's destroyed the goods on Seventh."

"Are we rolling out?" He adjusts his suit.

"Not you. I need you to protect my sister. Watch her with your life. Understood?"

He nods. "Yes, Damiano." If there's anyone I trust to watch my sister, it's him. The man is madly in love with her. He's been that way for the past six months, even if he doesn't know it himself. Gabriele would give his life for her, and that's what I need in a guard for her. Nothing less is acceptable.

I spot Gracie and Camille with my angel heading to the

exit. No, she's not my angel, and I need to remember that. She's too good for a monster like me, and I'll ruin her. Still, I can't let her ass go. "Ladies, before you go, Gabriele will escort you back."

"Really?" Camille says with a flirty smile, and I don't miss my sister's annoyance. Apparently, my underboss isn't the only one who is interested. I'll have to talk to both of them soon. I won't have them sneaking around behind my back.

"Yes, I will, but stop with the flirting act because it won't work. I don't like whores."

"Good girls don't have any fun. Ask my stepsister. She's getting married to an old man." She giggles and adds, "I need another drink. Oh, look, Stella, there's the guy who was buying you drinks. Maybe he'll give you a nice long ride home since we're leaving early." My eyes move to Ernesto, the slimeball ass, and I smile.

"Thank you, Camille," I say, leaving her confused, but Gabriele knows exactly what I have planned. Turning to my sister, I say, "Have a fun night, and remember what I said."

"Yes, Brother." Smartly, Grace leads Camille toward the exit while I drag Stella back a step.

Pulling her close, I whisper in her ear, "It's not over. You're mine, and I'm coming for you. When I do, there will be hell to pay for running away. Be prepared, Angel. You're not marrying anyone else." I bite her ear and then send her away with a pat on her ass. Even if I can't have her, no one else will be forcing her hand. She's not marrying him, and when I find out who he is, he'll pay with his life.

I tell my doorman to nab Ernesto; he and I have much to discuss later, and I'll take my frustration out on him.

CHAPTER EIGHT

STELLA

"Sorry about my brother being so strict, Stella. I know he didn't let you drink or anything," Gracie says, knowing damn well she walked in on me as I was rubbing my creaming pussy on her brother's lap, shaking out my first orgasm. She's doing what she can to hide the truth from Camille because my stepfather would end my life for the betrayal.

"It's okay. I'm not sure I'd know how to have fun," I lie, pretending to be unbothered when all I want to do is run back into his arms and beg him to save me, even if it's just to stop my wedding. He doesn't have to want me as long as he helps me run.

"That's for sure," Camille complains. "Is there any booze back here?" she asks, looking at Gabriele, who's driving us in a blacked-out SUV.

"No. Now sit back and relax. I think Rocco plied you with enough booze," he snarls. Both Gabriele and

Damiano don't like my stepsister, which I find interesting because they run a club with half-naked women dancing like strippers and getting wasted, so Camille doesn't seem any different, except that she's a bitch. Yes, I didn't get a good look at anyone in the club before we were dragged upstairs and I had the best and only orgasm of my life, but I'm feeling so confused right now. Who is Damiano Valentino?

"I have some more at the house anyway," Gracie whispers. I really like her, even if her brother is insane and intense. God, the feelings he pulled out of me are still electrifying my body.

"Good, because this night has been a bust. We spent more time getting ready than we did at the club." More can happen in that short time than in my entire life.

My heart races as I think about that brief moment in Damiano's arms. He made me feel wanted, craved, desired, and not just by some creepy old man. Damiano could have any woman he wanted. When his eyes landed on me, I couldn't help but drop my gaze. The intensity took over, and I wondered if the alcohol had gone straight through me.

Every cell in my body shook with desire, and then he took my hand in his and kissed it. I nearly slid right off the leather. By some miracle, I didn't embarrass myself and I remained glued to my seat.

We arrive at the house, security opening the gates. They have a small estate and once we're inside, I'm taken to a bedroom that I'll be sleeping in for the night. "Excuse me, but…"

"You can sleep in here. We'll be down the hall.

Goodnight." Gracie rushes Camille from the room, who doesn't give a shit about leaving me alone.

"Lead me to the booze," I hear Camille say.

I turn on the light and look around the room. It's clearly a man's bedroom, and instantly I know who it belongs to. This is his room, or at least his old room. Will he show up here? Is that why she left quickly? He's not going to be here for a long time because the club doesn't close for hours, so I decided to peek into his things. The entire room is pristine and manly, from the neat dresser to the perfectly made bed with cream and navy-blue bedding. I open his closet, and there are several suits lined up. Immediately, I find my face pressed to the fabric like a fool, breathing them in as if they haven't been laundered. Still, there's a hint of him in the closet.

Hearing footsteps outside the room, I quickly step out and move to the bed before I get caught. I slip off my shoes, slide out of my dress so that I'm just in my panties, and let my body collapse onto the mattress. His scent engulfs me as I wrap up in his sheets.

"Thank you, Gracie," I murmur as I wrap myself in his covers and rest my head on his pillows.

I don't want to sleep, but then again, I want to dream of Damiano. There's no way I'll see him again. He may say he wants to see me again and that I'm his, but he's a smooth talker—a man who probably takes pretty women up to his VIP lounge every chance he gets. That burns in my chest more than it should, considering my fate was sealed long before I met him.

I wake up the next morning, and Grace slips into the room. "Did you sleep well?"

"Um…yes," I murmur, covering myself up with the sheets.

"So…I hoped he'd stop by this morning, but I guess he's busy."

"Is that why you put me in here?" I question, giving her a wry smile.

"A sister can hope." She shrugs.

"Thanks, but I'm sure you read too much into last night."

"He said to make sure you were safe." My mouth falls open. "There's nowhere safer."

There's a thud as someone fiddles with the door handle. "Hey, why is this door locked?" Camille gripes behind the bedroom door.

"I'll be there in a moment," Grace calls out.

"My father wants Stella home in an hour," she shouts.

"Miss, please step away from the door."

"Is that Gabriele?"

"Yes." She nods and then turns to the door and says, "Okay. I'll drive you both home in twenty minutes."

"I meant just her. I can stay." Of course Camille doesn't want to leave this fabulous place; she probably wants to run into Damiano even though he doesn't like her.

"Yes, but I have somewhere to be." Grace looks at me and says, "Get dressed to go home." She walks to the bedroom door and then slides out, hitting the lock inside before going so Camille can't see inside. In the light of day, the room is beautiful and manly. I breathe in Damiano's room. As I go to change my clothes, I notice my panties have a pink stain on them, so I quickly change my clothes. *Damn him.* Well, he can keep them. When I use his en-suite, it's clear I don't have my period, so the Devil stole more than my first orgasm last night.

As I gather my things, I toss them in his top drawer and walk out of the room.

CHAPTER NINE

DAMIANO

I stare at the damage, ready to bust some heads, but all I can think about is the fact that Stella is marrying someone else. There are so many hands that can be paid off. We have those who looked the other way, and those who wanted to dig deeper. Tonight of all nights, I'm not going to get the right fucker.

The fire department has been all over the scene, putting out the blaze, and I saw the questions in their eyes when I arrived with my men. It was obvious the situation is going to be settled behind the scenes without official paperwork and arrests; still, they have statements to take.

"Hello, Mr. Valentino. Might I have a word with you?" Chief Fire Inspector Rodriguez asks. This guy is on the straight and narrow, a real fucking ball-buster, as it would seem, so depending on my mood, one of us might need help. He'll need a medic, and I might need a lawyer.

"Yes." We step toward his city-issued SUV, and my

men stay just feet away, on edge. "So, what can you tell me about this, Inspector?" I ask before he can start his line of questioning.

"Nothing, at the moment, other than it's contained. We'll know more in a few hours. Although, if it is arson, we ask that you allow the authorities to handle the matter." My brow cocks up. "I see that everything is falling on deaf ears."

"Do you know if anyone was inside?" I question, hoping there weren't any late back-end deals going on. If any of my men were killed, I'll go on a hunting party. It's been a long time since I've strung up carcasses by the dozen.

"Should there have been anyone inside?" He raises his brow, mouth creasing and laced with suspicion.

I don't let his snark bother me because he doesn't like my kind, and frankly, I don't like his do-gooder ass anyway. "No, there shouldn't have been anyone. However, you never know what happens when someone commits arson."

"I never said it was arson, only that it's a possibility, Mr. Valentino," he reminds me, brows raising with suspicion.

I lean in, anger getting the better of me. "My properties aren't prone to spontaneous combustion, Mr. Rodriguez." I feel Adriano's hands on my shoulders, reminding me of my actions. Straightening myself, I adjust my suit jacket and add, "Please keep me posted." This bastard hates me, and that's fine—as long as he gets me answers and minds his own business. It isn't like I lit the bitch on fire. I was in the middle of setting fire to Stella's veins while she burned her name into my soul and marked my skin with her breath, making me feel something I never expected. Something I need to push back before I do something stupid.

"We'll contact you if we have more questions. Just let us do our jobs."

"Make sure you do them properly, Inspector," I snarl.

"Is that a threat?"

"Why would I threaten a man like you? I was in the middle of the best night of my life when I was interrupted. Get this shit straightened out so our worlds are safer." I smile at the bastard and walk away. Unfortunately, there is nothing more I can do, so my men follow me to the club.

I call the head of security for the club. "Nico, get me the footage of the bar when my sister arrived. There should be footage of my sister's friends at the bar."

"Holly said you might want it."

"She's smart." I reach the club and walk up to the bar. Holly is serving a customer, so I wait a moment.

"Yes, Boss. A whiskey, neat?"

"Sure. How did you know I wanted the footage?"

"Camille's trouble, so I made an excuse not to serve them, and then you called them up there. When I saw Camille with just Rocco, I asked Sasha about the girl because I worried Ernesto would get his paws on her again. She told me she was safe upstairs with you."

"Paws on her again? Please elaborate."

"He grabbed her ass. It's probably on the video."

"What?" I question, setting my glass down without revealing the fury in my soul. Ernesto has earned himself a one-way ticket to hell, and I'm going to enjoy sending him there.

"Rocco told him that was a bad idea and dragged him away." That earned Rocco some fucking points with me, but he was still sitting too close to my angel when I walked in.

"Damn right. Thank you," I say before tapping the bar with a hundred and taking my glass.

The fucker thought he had a claim on my woman, and he was sorely mistaken. I enter the security room, and the video is cued up. The girls are at the bar, and my eyes are locked on Stella's ass, which is almost completely on display. Ernesto moves into view, blocking her, but then the camera angle switches and he's in her space, hoping to buy her a drink, which she clearly doesn't like, and Camille's trying to scam. His hands move on her the second Rocco arrives, and then he fucking cups her ass.

I punch the damn wall. Nico whispers in my ear, and I'm out the door. With a grin, I take the steps to my office two at a time. I was informed that Ernesto is waiting in my office. Round two.

My club has been emptied out for the night, and there will be no one to hear the screams. I slam the door to my office wide open, and my eyes drop to look for the cloth on the floor. Thankfully, my rug hasn't been put back in place. Lifting my gaze with a smile, I stare at my guest. "Mr. Valentino, I don't know why they're wasting your time. My date and I just..." My fist lands in his gut.

"Your date?" I questioned.

Adriano shakes his head at the fool. "Are you referring to the girl at the bar whose ass you grabbed?"

"Sorry. I didn't know she was with your sister." My hand goes to his face, breaking his nose. He cries like a little bitch, but I'm not done with him. Walking over to the wall, I hit a switch, then grab my weapon of choice and head to my guest.

Grabbing him by the throat, I stare him down. "You touched my woman. You put your filthy hands on my angel." I pull out my blade and slice off his hand. Blood gets everywhere, but luckily the guys are prepared. "This is the last time you'll stain my property with your stench." I jab the knife into his eye. "That's what you get for thinking she belonged to you." I pull the blade out, and then Adriano hands me a cloth.

Cleaning the knife, I glare at the piece of shit they're already wrapping up in the tarp. "Let that be a warning to everyone."

"Understood."

I head into my bathroom and strip out of my clothes, turning on the shower. Fuck, I need to get rid of this insane feeling coursing through me. Who the fuck is this Stella, and why is she affecting me like this?

Washing off all the blood, I ignore my raging hard-on and dress in a clean suit. When I step out, my office is spotless. I pick up my cell and call Gabe. "Give me an update."

"Grace is with her friends at your parents'. I'm outside the house, watching it. Do you want me to stay?"

"Go inside and take the sofa. No need to stay outside. We have security for that shit. Just watch out for that sneaky one."

"Don't worry. I think Gracie will toss her on her ass."

"How is…"

"I don't know. They went inside, and Gracie sent me packing. She's definitely not as soft as you think."

"We need to talk soon."

"Any problems?"

"No, everything's taken care of. Get some rest." I end the call before telling him because my father is his problem.

Now that I know she's safe in my family's home, I've decided to sleep at the club and let my temper cool before I even approach my sweet little Stella. There is no way I can face her with the rage boiling in me.

CHAPTER TEN

STELLA

My nerves are only more frazzled. One day left, and I'm not sure I can handle the pressure. Gracie dropped us off only two hours ago, so I don't know why she's back, torturing me with her presence. It's not that I don't like her. Hell, I think she's amazing and the polar opposite of Camille. It's just that I want to ask her about her brother, but Camille has monopolized her time the whole morning. She gave me a sheepishly apologetic smile when we were interrupted.

Since then, we've had guards lingering. Grace's guards linger by the door, which my stepfather remarks on. "We have strict orders by Mr. Valentino. She can leave if you'd prefer that, Sir," he snarls, but my stepfather quickly raises his hands and steps back, knowing that no one tells Mr. Valentino no. I don't know how we managed not to get caught by my stepfather's guards, or Tommy's, either. It's like we had the all-clear last night. A little too clear, which means they had it all planned out, except for Gracie's brother. Gracie's parents must be seriously dangerous people, or perhaps the Mr. Valentino he's referring to is her brother.

No, that's silly. I ignore that thought because it's just a girl's foolish dream. I almost expected Damiano to sneak into his bedroom and slide into bed with me, but that would be ridiculous because he hadn't shown up. I was all alone.

I sit in my bedroom, packing my bags for tomorrow, dreading my future or what I have left of it. There isn't much I can do about my life, but I have a choice I can make. It's mine, and at least it's my own.

There's a light rap on my door, so gentle that I almost don't hear it over my thoughts.

"Come in." It's not like I'm allowed to refuse entry to anyone in this house. The last time it occurred, I felt his wrath and lost my pillows for a week, all because I was changing my clothes and didn't open the door immediately. Of course, he didn't believe me and did a thorough search of my room for any deceit. Even after he didn't find any, he said it must be in my head so I deserved to be punished.

The door opens, and I'm surprised to see Gracie. "Hi," I say.

She presses her finger to her lips. "Hi. I came to check on you."

"Um…Thanks." I blow a strand of hair out of my face and carry on with my packing.

"Are you sure this is what you want?" she asks.

The absolute look of disgust on my face has to be

obvious because I can feel my face contort painfully. "What I want? Does it appear like I have a choice?"

"You always have a choice."

"Oh, I have a choice, all right. And I might take it." I hold up a giant pill bottle of old Tylenol. "One heavy dose, and all my troubles will be gone." Grace's face falls, and I give her a weak smile and shake my head. "I'm teasing."

"Mm-hmm. So…" She takes a seat on my bed. "Ouch. Damn, how old is this thing?" I don't mention that I've had this twin bed since I was a child. "Sorry, that's rude. So, is there anything I can do for you?"

Being bold, I state, "Tell your brother to keep his promise."

She smiles and lays her hand on mine, giving it a gentle squeeze. "No one tells Damiano what to do, but you should trust me when I say he keeps his word, so if he told you he would do something, he will." God, I hope so.

My door slams open, and Camille pops in with a menacing flash my way before smiling at her friend. "Gracie, what are you doing in here?"

She turns up a pretty grin at Camille that I've just registered as fake compared to the genuine one she gave me moments ago. "I'm checking on the bride-to-be, of course. You were all busy and everything."

"Sorry, girl. I didn't mean to leave you all alone." Wow, does she have to act like I'm not even standing right here? It's getting a bit ridiculous. "Well, let's go and hang out today."

"Actually, I have to go home now. My parents are getting back tomorrow, which means I need to be on my best behavior and catch up on my reading. They can be a real pain about my lack of mental enrichment, but that's why I came back for another quick visit. Maybe you could stop by next week after they settle in."

"Totally. I'm so glad my daddy doesn't get on me about reading. I'll walk you out." I ignore the both of them because Camille will get suspicious if Gracie gives me any more attention. I wonder if she knows about what happened between Damiano and myself that night at the club.

The second Gracie's gone, I'm absolutely right. Camille slams open my bedroom door. "Are you trying to steal my friend?"

"What? No," I gasp. "Are you nuts? I'm getting married, or have you forgotten."

"Oh, I haven't forgotten." She shuts my door, smiling the entire time. The wicked grin on her face reminds me that she's a total cunt and there's no redeeming qualities left in my stepsister. When we were younger, she wasn't totally evil, but now there's absolutely nothing remaining. I've always hoped that she would turn around and be my friend, and last night gave me a glimpse of hope that she might have had an ounce of empathy or compassion.

I drop on my hard, lumpy mattress and flattened pillow, wanting to suffocate myself, but I remain strong and hope that I can keep it together enough to give Damiano a chance to hold up his promise, although I'll deal with my problems if he doesn't show tomorrow.

One way or another, I won't be a victim to my stepfather and his friends ever again.

CHAPTER ELEVEN

DAMIANO

My sister bursts through my office door as if there's no security in my damn club. Luckily the club doesn't open for three more hours because I'd have to bust some heads. "Gracie, to what do I owe this unexpected surprise?" I ask, snarling at Gabriele, who holds the door open for her while standing back and refusing to look at me. *Pussy.*

She pops into the seat in front of my desk and interlaces her fingers, her usual bubbly demeanor a bit shaken and a cloud of darkness around her. "We need to talk."

"That sounds ominous, Hummingbird. Is this about a man?" A growl comes from the door. "You can close it, Gabe," I say, getting a scowl from him before he shuts the door behind him, leaving my sister and me alone. I do love the torture I'm putting him, through.

She bites her lip and sighs. "No, it's about Stella."

"What about Stella?" My temper rises. I haven't forgotten about her upcoming marriage; I was trying to find out who she is marrying, but the damn explosion from last night got in the way. The damn inspector is already on my ass with calls. I met with him, only for him to drill me with inane questions that could have been asked over the phone. He had nothing new to provide and only wanted to waste my time.

She stands up, and then sits back down. "I'm afraid that she'll kill herself if she marries Tommy Baker."

"What the fuck do you mean Tommy Baker?" I bellow. My sister jumps back like I was going to harm her, falling backward out of her chair. Her eyes are wide as I rush around and help her up off the floor. "I'm so sorry, Gracie. You know I'd never hurt you, Hummingbird."

"It's just…I've never seen that look in your eyes before. Well, at least directed at me."

"I'm sorry. It's not directed at you," I snarl, clenching my teeth.

"The proverbial 'don't kill the messenger'?" she eeks out, rubbing her elbow.

I cup her chin. "Never, dearest. Run along. I promise she won't be marrying that slime. In fact, if everything goes well, you will be getting a sister, but you must keep it to yourself."

That softens the brutal fear I put in her for the first time. "Of course. I'm a Valentino. Everything is a secret, Brother. I love you."

I kiss the top of her head and then add, "Love you, too, Hummingbird. Now, have Gabriele escort you out, and then tell him to see me immediately."

She walks to the door and says, "Oh, by the way—I let her sleep in your bed."

"You did?"

She nods with a smile and flits away, a lightness in her step that had been missing when she entered my office. Was she truly scared to tell me, or scared for Stella?

I stand and walk straight to the built-in bar against the right wall where I keep my top-shelf booze, pouring myself a glass of whiskey and shooting it down. It goes down smoothly, so I chase it down with a second. Setting my glass on the wooden top, I walk away before the whole bottle is polished off.

My feet move without me realizing it, sending me pacing back and forth, murderous thoughts racing through my head.

Tommy Baker? That's who the fuck she's marrying? That fucking sick old bastard? The fucking loser who borrowed a million dollars from me last month? Is this why he asked for the money? My angel. That would never happen. I'll kill that bastard.

A rapid knock on my door before someone enters startles me, and I whip out my gun to find Gabriele staring at me. "Whoa, whoa. Chill."

I tuck my gun back in and then run my hand through my disheveled hair. "What the fuck? Why are you just bursting through the door?"

He throws his hands up and closes the door. "You summoned me, and then didn't answer your door."

"I just heard you knock."

"I've knocked three times. What's going on, Dame?" I

stare at my friend a second and wonder how the hell I didn't hear him. Do I need my ears checked?

"Baker is fucking marrying my…Stella." I almost call her my angel, when she's not. As much as I crave her, she can't be anything more than something I lust after. Lust… fuck, I never lust after anything but the blood of my enemies. Why has she done this to me? She's a fragile little thing that needs a protector, not the devil.

"No, for real? Gracie's little friend?" he says, twisting his lips in a smirk.

"Yes. The nerve of that fucking piece of shit." My fists clench at my sides, flexing until my nails dig into my palms.

"But you're not letting that happen, right?" he asks, walking to my bar to pour himself a drink.

"Of course not." He knows what I did to Ernesto, even though he didn't witness it.

"Do you want a drink?" he asks.

I wave him off. "I've had enough."

"What's your game plan?"

"I'm going to fucking blow his brains out, but not before I demonstrate my power over the bastard." Normally I'm cool, rational until I hear something I don't like, and this is something I hate—despise. Tommy Baker stealing something so precious shouldn't even be a thought, and yet he was about to if I don't do anything about it.

I seethe with rage as I imagine his hands all over her: caressing her soft skin like I had, tasting her lips, drinking in her scent, worshiping her sweet innocence, and ruining her. No, he'd break her, and if anyone was going to darken her light, it belonged to the devil. She belongs to me.

"What about her?"

"I'll make sure she doesn't marry him." With a nod of his head, he tosses back his drink, and I consider how I'm going to make this happen.

After a long day, I stopped back at my parents' home and went into my bedroom. Like a wonderful sister, she didn't tell the staff to clean my room after our guest was here. My first stop is my bed where I bring my pillow to my face. "Fuck me." My dick is hard against the expensive fabric of my briefs. I groan as I breathe her in and try to control the urge to pull my cock out. I'm too grown to give in to a quick masturbation just because she slept in my bed, or so I tell myself. A knock at my door catches me by surprise. I dropped the pillow and yanked my boxer briefs back in place, forgetting how hard I was.

"What is it?" I grit through clenched teeth, pissed at myself and whoever is at the door because not only did I not get off, but now I'm in pain.

"Brother?" Son of a bitch. Of all the people to be at the door, it has to be my little innocent sister.

I slam my eyes shut as I try to get my breathing under control enough to respond properly. "One moment, Gracie." Sliding out of bed with I adjust my cock and then go to the door, unlocking it and letting her in.

"I didn't expect to see you here. Everything okay?" she asks, giving me a concerned once over. *Fuck, come on, kid.* Luckily it's dark in the room and the blackout curtains are closed.

"Yes. I'll be making some moves tomorrow. Drastic moves that require you to attend a wedding with me."

"A wedding?"

"Yes, I'd like to go over the details. I hope you have something beautiful to wear tomorrow."

"I don't want to celebrate it."

"Trust me, Hummingbird. Stella won't be marrying that piece of shit." She throws her arms around me, and I have to push her to the side.

"Sorry, I was sleeping."

"No problem, kiddo." She thinks it's because she's in her PJs, but it's because I've been fantasizing about what I want to do to her friend. "Go to bed, since we have a big day tomorrow."

"Perfect." She squeals and runs off to her room.

I set the alarm on my phone and then strip down to shower. When I come out, I open my underwear drawer and find an unexpected surprise.

"Fuck me. What a surprise, Stella." I stare at my trophy with dark pride. Tucking them away, I slip on a clean pair of boxers before sliding under the covers. Thoughts of why she put them in the drawer run through my head, driving me wild and stiffening my dick. I run my hand over my length and then stop, trying to fight the urge to beat off—to save all my arousal for tomorrow.

CHAPTER TWELVE

DAMIANO

When we pull up to the venue, I'm a little perplexed. Pissed is the better word as I try to fight this irrational pull toward Stella. Given the forced nature of the ceremony and all, I'm surprised Baker's trying to make this actually appear legitimate. Maybe he's looking for real investors. We'll be taking a list of RVSPs so I'm aware of who welcomed this union, although Gracie and Gabe are making moves as we speak to stop guests from entering the church.

Adriano and I step up to Tommy's door and barge in. "Hello, Tommy. I hear you're getting married," I say, dressed in my best suit. His mouth falls open in pure shock, giving himself a triple chin and nearly suffocating himself with his bowtie.

Staring at this man, I do my best to hide my disgust at the poorly fitted suit. Couldn't he have had it tailored to fit since he has my money and is attempting to marry an angel?

My men have already put my plan in motion. Tommy doesn't know what's coming, but it won't be him. My men are all waiting in the wings for what I have planned. Her stepfather's fate will be delayed, but Tommy's will soon come. The thought of him putting his mouth on my woman is enough to send me over the edge. I could slit his throat now, but his presence is required for this next part.

Has he seen her after I had my first taste? Did he enjoy her scent now tainted with mine? Well, it won't matter because he won't get that close to touching her again.

"Yes. You didn't get my invite?" he finally chokes out, grabbing his collar and stretching it for air. Air that will soon leave his body after I've enjoyed tormenting him.

"No. Somehow, I didn't. I didn't even get a call to ask if I'd received it. Strange. I thought we were friends, Tommy." I knew it wasn't true, considering the man is late on my money.

"Must have been an oversight by the wedding planner and my bride. She can be a little absentminded." My ass. The poor girl doesn't have a say in how she fucking breathes. Interesting how his lies can come out so effortlessly when he thinks he's safe here.

"Mistakes like that can happen," I answer, letting my perturbed mood show, although he doesn't know why.

"I understand that I still owe the money, but can we…"

"We can discuss that matter later. It's a wedding day," I say with a smirk, clapping my hand on his shoulder.

"Please do join us for the ceremony. It will be starting

soon. My bride is getting ready as we speak." Although I already knew it, the thought perturbed me.

"Oh, she is?" I'm seething internally, even if my expression doesn't give away an ounce of my tension. The idea of her preparing to marry another man pisses me off so badly that I want to snap his neck right on the spot, but he deserves more than a quick death.

"Yes, but you know women. She'll probably just be finished as the music begins to play."

I chuckle because there will be no bridal march. "I can't stay, but I must meet her and wish her congratulations. Please escort me to her room. I'll be quick." He's hesitant but knows that I'm not asking. This isn't a request.

We take the stairs, and unlike him, my guards are trained killers. He has no idea what lies ahead. My men stay alert. Rocco and Adriano move in step behind me, ready for my plan to be in action. The wedding doesn't start for another hour so most of the guests haven't even arrived, and those who have are being escorted out with the knowledge that the bride has developed *cold feet* and has called off the wedding.

As they are quietly being removed, her stepfather is in his dressing room getting hammered with one of my guards watching. He is too poor to hire his own guards, and Tommy's have already been dispatched. Stella's stepsister is in the room with her, which is a precarious situation that will soon be rectified. I don't trust that bitch armed with a piece of paper in front of Stella. She'd try to give her a paper cut.

Knock, Knock. Tommy bangs his fat knuckles on the

door with his pinky ring, scuffing the wooden surface. "One minute."

I stand off to the side with my back to the door so her evil stepsister can't recognize me. "I need to see Stella," Tommy says.

"She's not in her dress, so that's cool. Although not that it matters. The dumb bitch doesn't have a chance and you're her only choice." She steps out and heads down the hall to where her father's getting wasted.

It's rare that a female ends up on the radar for disposal, but Camille has crossed a line. She drugged Rocco, and the tests proved it. He'd been high as a kite and under her influence, so dealing with her demise is something he wants to handle personally. She nearly cost him his life, and he is pissed. After what she said about Stella, there is no love lost where they are concerned. She has to go.

I turn around, following Tommy into her dressing room. Gouging his eyes out is going to be fun.

"Stella, I'd like you to meet a friend of mine." She has her back to us, clad in a beautiful, silky white robe that does little to hide her sensuously round bottom and slender back. Even from this view, she's gorgeous and way out of this fucker's league. My body's reaction is instant, and I can't wait to peel it off her. Fuck me. I'm hard just staring at her slight frame and perfect curves.

"If he's a friend of yours, he's not worth meeting," she says with much venom, deepening my arousal. I'm proud of her.

"You little bitch," Tommy snarls, lunging forward, but Adriano has him with his hands behind his back before he can go after my woman. Tommy yelps like a little bitch.

"Now, is that any way to speak to an angel?" She gasps and turns around. Her eyes widen at the sight of me with her hand going to her chest. Immediately my eyes glue to the fucking bullshit ring on her finger. It's the first time I've seen it on her, and a new, profound rage I hadn't expected to feel courses through my veins.

"Mr. Valentino," she says, eyes wide in shock as if she hadn't expected to see me.

"You're asking for that spanking, Stella." She wants to pretend we're not on more familiar terms. Does she think this bastard is somehow more powerful than me? Or he has some way to keep her from me?

"That's no way to speak to my fiancée, Mr. Valentino." I whip my head around in a flash and stare at him like he's nuts.

"That's ten," I breathe out through clenched teeth as I backhand the bastard.

"What are you doing here? I told you I was getting married," she says, emphasizing that last bit, adding fuel to the fire of my rage.

"Eleven." My teeth are clenched tighter than my fists at the moment.

She tilts her pretty head, eyes questioning. "Eleven?"

I stalk toward my bride, watching her move back toward the settee. "Yes—the times that someone reminded me that he made a deal to buy your hand. Frankly, nobody tells me something I don't like to hear more than once." I turn to him and glare. "Everyone knows that."

When I look back at my bride in her white robe, it only amplifies the fact that she was hours from letting him take her to his bed. "See, I warned you what would happen if you ran. Now, see, we have a serious problem... you're looking good... except for this." I take her hand in mine and yank off the fake diamond, tossing that shit across the room and watching it shatter on the floor.

She gasps and looks up into my eyes. I cup her face, brushing a few strands of loose hair away from her eyes. "See? It's a piece of shit, baby girl. He bought you with my money and couldn't even spoil you with it."

"Your money?" she gasps, rose-red lipstick marring her puffy lips—the pretty mouth that should be wrapped around my cock, pleasing me daily like I woke up this morning dreaming about. My balls ache to feel her gagging on my length until I spend down her throat.

I grasp her chin, staring into her eyes. "Yes. He borrowed my money to buy you. Do you know what that means?" Of course, even if she doesn't, it won't matter because she is mine.

She shakes her head without freeing herself from my hold. "That means you're mine."

"No, it doesn't," Tommy growls from his tied-up state in the corner of the room, like he has a voice in this situation. He wants to act tough, but there are thirteen-year-old kids that have lived on the street with more balls than this fucker.

I ignore the bastard because he doesn't matter. "It means I get to finish what we started."

"Started?" he questions with a sense of betrayal in his voice. I almost crack up laughing at his response.

She shakes her head, but the look in her eyes tells me otherwise. She looks over to Tommy and I snarl, feeling irrationally more jealous than a motherfucker. There's no reason for it because I know she doesn't want to marry him, but still, she's deferring to him.

Gracie told me what was in Stella's wedding bag, and that unsettled me. My girl is planning to kill herself if she has to go through with the wedding, so this pussy has nothing on me. Gracie said she played it off as a joke, but we both knew that shit wasn't. It takes more courage to die than live a life of brutality. Not that I'd ever let that happen. My job is to bring her pleasure, and we're going to do it while tormenting her tormentors. Even though I'm no good for her, it's better than losing such an angel on this earth.

"Mouth, now," I growl. She shakes her head as she licks her lips. "You either kiss me now, or I'll make you drop to your knees and suck me off right in front of this asshole. Do you want that? Do you want him to see you please me?" Her chest heaves through the silky material, eyes filled with a wicked light. I grip her hair, pulling on her updo. "Do you want him to watch as you get on your knees and wrap those red lips around my thick fucking cock?" She parts those plump beauties, gasping, slamming her silky thighs closed. That's what I want to see.

I tug on her robe, freeing it and seeing her in just a pair of lace panties and bra. Adriano, having tied up Tommy, smartly turned around. "Open up." She does, and I slide my tongue into her mouth before kissing her hard. Breaking our kiss, I smirk and kiss the tip of her nose. "Such a good girl, but I'm not satisfied, Angel."

"What do you need, Damiano?" she asks.

I grab a pillow off the settee and set it on the floor, then press on her shoulders, forcing my sexy angel down to her knees. "Free my cock, now." She looks up at me with needy blue eyes, and I can't fight how wrong this is. Claiming her in front of him is all I can think about.

"Fuck, she's mine," Tommy whines like the little bitch that he is.

"No, she's mine. I paid for her. Remember that." Blood pounds in my ears as I consider that she was what he wanted my money for. I tug on her hair a little harder, wanting to show everyone I'm still in control, but I'm hanging on by a thread.

Looking down at my angel, I command, "Suck." My cock comes out from my clothes, and she hesitantly takes me between her candy-red lips. "So damn sweet," I growl as she takes the first lollipop lick, and then she slides her mouth up and down my length, learning how to take more and more with each bob of her head. Her teeth scrape my dick, and I'm tempted to wrap my hand around her throat and see her gag. Fuck, I'm so horny.

"Damn. Don't bite me, or I'll fuck that tight hole right in front of your ex-fiancé," I snarl through the pleasure of her sensual torture.

"Oops, that's twelve," Adriano blurts out with a chuckle. The smartass is going to get a bonus for that one. Stella sucks me down, taking my cock deep down her throat, working my length over and over. A moan falls from her lips as she grows more confident. My hand slides down her chest and under the lace cup, rubbing her hardened nipple.

She moans around my cock, and I can't hold on any longer. I'm about to come when there is a knock at the door. Pulling my massive hard rod out of her hot mouth,

I'm pleased to see I've ruined her lipstick. Caressing her cheek, I say, "We'll have to save this for later."

Quickly I tuck my cock back into my slacks and help my bride-to-be onto her feet, adjusting her robe back in place. I let myself get carried away when I have plans other than her blowing me in front of Baker. Once we're covered, I call Rocco and say, "Wedding bells."

"On it," he replies. I end the call and tuck my phone away.

I give Stella my attention. "A change of plans. Looks like you're still getting married today."

"I don't want to," she exclaims, glaring at me. I feel irrational anger. She's willing to marry that asshole, but not me? Well, that's tough shit because she is.

"Too late. The priest is here." Adriano holds a knife to Tommy's throat while keeping his hands tied.

"Father, please come in and marry us."

"Us?" She looks up at me in surprise. I thought I made that pretty damn clear, but maybe she wasn't sure of my intentions.

"Of course, 'us.' Did you think I'd let you marry that scum?" Her robe slips, and I feel jealousy permeate my brain. I'm going to kill Tommy, so I don't care if he sees her in a bra, and both of my men were turned around again, so I quickly slid her robe back in place.

"Is it time for us to come into the room?" Gracie asks from the doorway.

"Yes, Hummingbird."

"Stella," she squeals. "We're going to be sisters." She hugs my bride, who awkwardly gives in to the embrace. Yeah, my sister doesn't know that I just had my angel on her knees giving me a blow job. Fuck, I'm so hard. I can't wait to get my bride alone.

"Enough. Save it for later. We need to get going." My blue balls can't wait much longer.

Tommy grunts and fights. "You can't have her."

"Keep that fucker quiet, or get him out of here."

"Okay." Andriano pulls tape out of his coat and covers Tommy's mouth to keep it shut.

"Father Santos, please continue with the ceremony." We rush through the service with my sister tucking a blue flower clip into Stella's hair, although I already have something blue—a pair of somethings.

The second we're pronounced husband and wife, I slide my ring on my wife's hand. Her eyes widened. Leaning in for her ears alone, I whisper, "This is real, and I expect you to never take it off or I'll tan your ass." The ring was a last-minute item I picked up from my father's favorite jeweler on the way. He had bought my mother so many pieces that I was guaranteed a quick turnaround with the request I made in the early morning hours after the fire, even down to the inscription. Luckily, her size is pretty standard, and it fits on her slender hand. I bring her delicate hand to my lips and kiss the piece.

I lead her out of the little chapel with my sister and Gabe arm-in-arm. Rocco will bring our other special guests who missed the ceremony, while Adriano will handle our ex-bridegroom to be handled.

"Take my sister home. We'll do dinner later to celebrate." Gabe nods, and then I lead my bride into our waiting limo. As soon as the door closes, I smile as I realize I've won. Before I can kiss her, she slaps me across the face.

My fingers wrap around her wrist to stop her next one. "What the hell was that for?"

"Do you get off on a show?" she challenges me. She would have known if I got off. My nut would have been down her throat and all over her face.

I grip her by the throat, pinning her to the back seat. "No, and the evidence is clear since you're not tasting or wearing my load, but I warned you about running away. I would have fucked you in front of everyone if I didn't want anyone seeing you naked or hearing you come."

She tips her chin, brow arched without any fear in her ocean eyes. "I came quite loudly in the club."

I chuckled and release my grip. "The place was deafening, and we were isolated."

"Sorry, I forgot you're used to your party spot."

"Enough of your shit." I lift her up on my lap and slide my fingers over her wet opening. "I'm about to fuck you right now for that smart mouth of yours. You drive me insane, woman. I never let anyone speak to me the way you do."

"He's going to come after me." She tries to look out the back window, but I turn her head to focus back on me where it should be.

"That pussy isn't going to be breathing soon." I don't want to talk about any of this when I have the most beautiful creature in the world in my arms and half naked.

"What?" she gasps, pressing her hand to her sexy mouth that I want back on me.

"I told you; no one gets away with disrespecting me." I run my hand up her bruised arm.

"You're going to kill him?"

"Yes, and your stepfather too."

"Who are you?"

"You married a real mafioso, not like those fucks you lived with. Tommy was a businessman with a complex and no ambition. Now—enough talk about that. I want my wife to come here and let me show her all the pleasure she was begging for." My mouth lands on hers. At first she's hesitant, fighting it, and then she calms down, melting into it as her body relaxes. Her kisses deepen, and as my tongue slips inside her mouth, she clings to me.

I want to fucking breed her in the back of the vehicle, but I'll wait until we're in our bed. Hell, if my sister hadn't been at the wedding, I would have kicked everyone out and fucked my woman right on the settee for good measure.

CHAPTER THIRTEEN

STELLA

Married. I'm married to Damiano, and I'm trying to process it. My heart raced the second he entered the room because I knew I'd been saved, but then he wanted so much more. How can I be his wife? We don't know each other, and like he confessed, he's so much worse than the men who held my life in their hands.

He came, like he said. I can't think about what he said he'd do to my stepfather and Tommy. They both deserve it, but it's not something I'm capable of witnessing. He's dark and insane, but I can't pull away and I don't want to.

I ride his lap all the way to his home, feeling his thick length against my bottom. Even though my head is reeling with everything he revealed, I can't fight the driving lust pouring through me. When he had me drop to my knees in front of Tommy, I felt power flood me. I was showing the bastard that he didn't own me. I wasn't his.

Damiano made it seem like he was forcing me, but I could see in his eyes there was always a choice. The way he touched me was too tender, and yet hungry at the same time. I missed him so much that I eagerly wanted to kiss him when I turned around to see him standing in front of me. I didn't want to run away from him.

"Good, because I won't let you go." Oh, shit. I said that out loud. "Come on. It's time to take you inside and show you your new home."

"My new home?" Wow. My mouth gapes open with surprise at the magnitude of his estate. It's larger than his parents' mansion.

"Yes, of course. You're my wife." *Wife.* This is all shocking, overwhelming, and I'm starting to freak out. I never expected my life to do a full one-eighty. Yes, Damiano is a criminal just like my stepfather and my ex-fiancé, but at least he wants to please me. I still, freezing in place. Fear engulfs me with the state of my new reality. For how long? Will he grow tired of me and start abusing me? Or leave me for his club to screw his women like he had me on the seat or in his office.

"What's going on in that pretty head of yours?"

He stares at me, reading me all too well. "What do you mean?"

"You froze. It's too late to back out now."

"I don't know what you mean."

"Bullshit. You're trying to figure out if this was a mistake. You were going to marry that piece of shit. Marrying me can't be worse than him."

I shake my head and take the hand he has proffered out. The jolt of electricity vibrates through me, but I hide my reaction. "Show me the house, or rather, the mansion. Seriously, how many people live here?"

"Inside the house, my housekeeper is the only one. Most of the men live on property around the estate or nearby. As you know, my parents live not too far away."

"Oh, yes, I remember." I blush because I wasn't just sleeping in a guest bedroom that night. I'd been in his bedroom, resting my head on his pillow, under his covers, dreaming of him on his sheets.

"You have no idea how hard it was to stay away. If I didn't have business, I would have been sneaking into my parents' house and into my old bedroom like a creature of the night, devouring your sweet body until you were begging me to keep you."

"That's where you were?" Shit, I gave myself away.

"Yes, my angel." He brushes his lips against my temple. I turn and look up at him, and he freezes. Before I can react, he pulls me in for a kiss. Goodness, my entire soul embraces his hold on me as he makes love to me with his mouth. He's such an expert with his touch that I fall apart with a simple kiss, my walls breaking effortlessly. Damiano is truly talented and more dangerous than all the other predators I've known before, because he easily lures me in and I forget that I should run away.

He steps back slightly and looks at my lips. "That's a great look on you."

"What look?" I sigh, clinging to his chest.

"Desirous and hungry." The heat between my legs amplifies. I'm soaked with need. My lace panties are doing no good holding back the wetness. I'm about to make a puddle soon if I don't get some relief.

"Will you show me your bedroom?" I ask, giving up all pretense.

He taps my ass. "Our bedroom."

"Our bedroom," I repeat, biting down on my bottom lip, blushing in the process.

"So fucking sexy. The tour can wait. I need to strip you bare and finally claim you. It's been two days, and I can't wait any longer." He scoops me up in his strong arms, carries me up the stairs like a madman, and rushes into a bedroom, kicking the door closed behind him.

"You weren't kidding."

"Don't joke about anything, Stella," he growls, voice thick and heavy with need. He sets me down before taking the ties to my robe and tugging them free. The silk falls to the floor, pooling at my feet.

He pulls out a knife, eyes darkened with an angry glint to them. "These have to go. You wore them for someone else."

I shake my head, staring at those dangerous, territorial orbs. "No, I wore them for you."

His brows raise, questioning me. "What?"

"I hoped you'd come."

"What if I hadn't?"

"He was never going to see me in them." I remember the bag and the bottle. Swallowing hard, I put that sick thought out of my head because he came and there was no need for my plans.

"Then, my wife, strip for me. Show me what you have for your husband. I've stolen you, and I want you to show me what I get." He tucks the blade away in a drawer next to the bed before sliding off his suit jacket, and then he sits on the bed in front of me. "Now, Mrs. Valentino. It's time to show me what I don't deserve but have taken with sinful pleasure."

I should be nervous, but Damiano makes me feel alive, and I'll do whatever I can to get that high again and again. Arching my throat, I tilt my head, letting it roll once as I pull out the pin Gracie put in my hair and let the rest of my hair cascade over my shoulders.

He groans. "Fuck." His cock twitches in his gray slacks, so he undoes his belt, opening the top button.

I bite my lip and then reach in front where my bra clasp is and pop it open. My decently large breasts spill free, and he lets out a rapid succession of curses and praises while removing his clothes. I'm heated all over as I brush my hands over my chest and work lower down to my panties.

I don't get to slide them down before he's on me, lifting me onto the bed and setting me on my back with his strong body pinning me to the mattress. Our mouths meet in a frenzied kiss, lips connecting hard and fast, tongues sliding inside and dancing together with heated need. My hands thrust into his short black hair, tugging and pulling, turning his head all around while he grinds his hips forward. Then he suddenly pushes off me.

"What?"

"I need to eat your sweet cunt. It's been on my mind since we met, and I won't stop until I have that hot slit on my tongue. You only gave me a taste before you ran from me. I would have spread you wide and devoured your sopping wet cunt until you were screaming my name that night." I hadn't wanted to leave. I dreamed about him eating me out over and over again, sliding his tongue across my sensitive nub while I begged him to let me come.

Snaking his broad body down my tiny one, he looks up at me, eyes darker and mouth curling up with a wicked smirk. "Mine." The one word is all I need to feel another gush of fluid slide between my lower lips. He cups my breasts, running his tongue along the underside of each one before working his way to his goal. My hungry husband wants my pussy so bad; he grips my panties and with a quick tug, they're torn right off.

"Oops."

"I don't have any clothes," I remind him.

"Good. You naked is a gorgeous sight." His voice gets deeper, and my slit gives another pearl of liquid for him to drink up. I can't hide my desire for this man. Damiano grabs my calves and parts my thighs, settling his upper body right between them. "You smell so damn good, baby girl." He runs his nose along my mound before his mouth latches onto my pussy, and I arch my back right off the mattress, springing upward.

"Oh my God."

He chuckles and says, "God's not here. The devil only. I'm going to hell for corrupting an angel."

"Yes, that's right. Dame. Oh." I cling to the sheets for dear life. My feet dig into the mattress as I feel him push a finger into me. His thick tongue flattens over my hole, hitting every sensitive spot. "I'm going to come."

"Come for me, Angel. Come on my tongue."

He pumps his finger into me, then adds a second one and I'm losing my head, shaking. I grab his head, pressing his face into my pussy, rubbing it while I scream his name. My thighs shake as I orgasm wildly. This is so much more intense than the first time, and then he slowly rises up, looking dark and dangerous.

"Stella, are you ready to give your husband that tight pussy?"

"Yes."

"Wife, answer me properly."

"Yes, Husband."

"Good. Damn, that sounds so fucking good." His cock presses at my entrance, and then he pushes his way through. Even though he popped my cherry at the club with his hand, I'm being stretched painfully with his thick cock.

"Breathe, baby girl."

"You're so big. I thought it would be easier."

"I only broke your cherry. You have to get used to me. I'm not a small man," he says. He rocks slowly, and little by little I get used to his size. We move together, thighs rubbing, hips grinding as sweat beads down our bodies. My skin's tingling, and then I feel it right where I experienced it before.

"That's it, my angel. Let me hear you. Don't be shy. I want to hear those moans that were muffled between your sexy thighs." Right on cue, his fingers slide between us and he runs them over my little bud, rubbing it while taking my mouth in a kiss. "Fuck, your pussy is unbearably tight, Stella. So fucking tight." He grinds his hips, rocking in and out, dragging that massive length through me and I slam my eyes shut, trying to fight off my orgasm, but the man sends desire with every stroke like he was made just for me. It can't be right. He's sinfully bad, and I need to control this, yet I can't. Pleasure vibrates through my body. Damiano's head drops to my throat. "Wife, get out of that head. Stay with me and open those sexy eyes like you opened those luscious thighs."

"Damiano, it's happening again," I breathe against his mouth as we break for air.

"Good. Come for me because you're killing me. I'm doing my best, but your tight pussy is irresistible."

"I'm coming again," I cry out, nails digging into his back.

"Good girl, because I need to fuck this hole." He roars his need, and I feel his release filling me up as we move in time and slow down. "Perfect." He wipes the sweat from my brow and then kisses me again. I can't stop smiling when he slips out of me and then pulls me into his arms and holds me tight.

"Today wasn't like I expected."

"It was better than I expected."

"Oh yeah? Did you think I would be terrible in bed?"

"No, I didn't know if you'd let me have you."

"You would have waited if I wanted?"

"Of course. It would have drove me more insane than normal, but I'm not into rape." He brushes his lips against my temple. "Although if you'll excuse me, I do have some matters that need my attention. While we've been here, our guests have been waiting."

"I don't have any clothes."

"Oh, sweetheart, these guests you won't be seeing again. My sister will bring you clothes later. For now, rest." I close my eyes and pretend that I'm not bothered by what he just said. He's going to go kill people after just fucking me like it's not a big deal. Then again, it's my abuser and my buyer, so I can't really be upset that my husband would want to make them pay.

"Is my stepsister one of them?" I ask, wondering if he plans to kill her too.

"Would it matter if she was one of them?" he questions, dressing in sweats. Why does he look good dressed in such basic clothes?

"I don't know." I shrug.

"I'm not doing anything to her. As much as I'd love to snap her neck, I've had enough of her touch on my skin to last a lifetime. Sleep." He walks out of our bedroom. His words hit me like a truck—he's fucked my stepsister. My stomach turns, and I'm out of the bed and into the bathroom, vomiting violently.

CHAPTER FOURTEEN

DAMIANO

After getting dressed, I call Gabriele and check in. He's with Gracie at my parents' home, waiting for word to return here. "Give me the rundown."

"I haven't heard from Rocco yet. I called him four times since we left, but I assume he has his hands full moving the fuckers to the proper area, and once there, the signal cut out."

"Fuck. The signal fades in and out once you reach a specific range from the site, so we shouldn't expect to get word. Still, I don't believe that's the issue. Did he lose his nerve?"

"Do you think he'd turn on us for that cheap pussy?"

"Adriano is waiting for me. Bring Gracie so she can help Stella dress for dinner."

"I am. God, your sister has packed enough clothes that your wife isn't going to need anything for months."

"I doubt it. I'm sure she'll find a reason to take Stella shopping within a week." Gabe chuckles.

"We're loading the vehicle in five minutes. Shit."

"What is it?"

"Your parents just pulled up."

"Well, I guess dinner will have to be delayed. Inform them to join us in an hour, but bring Gracie because my wife needs clothes now."

"Okay, Dame." Fuck. They weren't supposed to be back for two more days. I'm going to get an earful from my father because of my mother. They have no idea that I'm not in love with my bride. This was just transactional. A debt that needed to be paid.

I turn around and go back into my bedroom, deciding to change into proper dinner wear, but the sound of Stella retching her brains out takes me by surprise. "What the fuck, Angel?"

She ignores me, which pisses me off because I'm trying to take care of her—something not in my wheelhouse. "What's wrong?"

Whipping her head in my direction, she wipes her mouth and glares at me with such fucking disgust you'd think I didn't just rock her world and have her screaming the house down. "You make me sick. Get away from me."

Holy hell. What fucking split motherfucking personality shit is going on here? A sense of indignation strikes me. I'm giving her more than she could ever dream of, including blissful orgasms, and this is how she repays me. "Damn. You didn't seem too upset when you were crying out my name."

"That's before I found out you were fucking my stepsister."

My head whips back like she slapped me. Wrapping a hand around her biceps, I lift her off the ground. "I should wash your filthy mouth out for saying something like that, but since you're punishing yourself, I suppose it's fair. I never fucked her."

"You said—" I press my fingers to her mouth, stopping whatever is about to be uttered and correct whatever misconception she has running in her head.

"I said no such thing. She put her hand on my chest attempting to flirt with me, and I was tempted to break it. Instead, I removed it with a warning."

"Oh." Her gorgeous pale cheeks turn bright pink with embarrassment.

"It's cute that you're jealous." My wife doesn't need to be jealous of anyone. I have romantic feelings for no one and only lustful desire for her.

Her eyes turn to slits as she glares at me. "It's not jealousy. It's disgusting. Of all the people in the world…" For her, that must have been a truly sickening thing. If I didn't care for the woman, Stella must hate her. She moves to the sink and washes her mouth.

I chuckle, which only pisses Stella off more. She stands up straight, and I swear she's ready to lunge at me. I raise my palms and shake my head. "Trust me. I feel the same way. Now, you need to wash up because my sister will be here shortly with clothes, and my parents will soon follow."

"Your parents?" Her pretty mouth humorously falls

open. She looks down at her naked form, and so do I. A groan rips from my throat.

"Yes." Damn, I've never been repeatedly hard. Fixing my growing erection, I kiss her forehead. "My sister is at the gate with Gabriele." I pull my robe from the back of the door and bring it to her. "I don't want anyone seeing you unclothed."

She points to the clothes on the floor. "My robe is over there."

"All of that will be burned."

"You mean my wedding gown?" she teases, pressing her hand to her chest as if it's a treasured relic. "How will I ever pass it down?" The eye roll is an unwelcome added touch.

"Brat. Remember—just because I enjoy that pussy doesn't mean I'll put up with that mouth."

"Great—from one abuser to another," she mutters.

I inch closer, wanting to take her over my knee to turn that sexy ass red. Fuck, my dick likes that idea. "What did you say?" I ask, wanting her to repeat it.

"Nothing, Mr. Valentino. I'll behave."

"Somehow I doubt that, Angel, but I don't mind bending that pretty ass over and spanking it before slamming my big cock in your tight cunt." She flushes a hot pink again. Tapping her cheek just as I hear footsteps in the distance, I say, "Don't get too worked up, baby. We have company."

"Dame, we're here. We hope you two are decent," Grace shouts from the stairway.

I exit the bathroom and then leave my bedroom to greet my sister and take the luggage from Gabe. "Go inside and help Stella pick something to wear."

My eyes go wide when I see my mother behind my sister. "Sorry. You know damn well I couldn't tell your father no," Gabe says. Of course, he wouldn't dare, and I couldn't either. I may be the Don, but my father is still a powerful man and a man we all respect.

"Of course," I mutter. "Where is my father?"

"Waiting for you in your study."

I set down the suitcases and wrap my mother in a hug. "Welcome back, Mother."

"Yes, I'm sure you're glad I'm back, Son." She slaps me in the chest. "Married?"

"It's not what you think."

"No? You don't have a wife?"

"It's not like we got married for love. That would never happen." She frowns and then looks around my shoulder at my door.

"So, are these for me?" Stella's voice comes from behind me. My eyes slam shut because even if I know the words are true, it still makes me an asshole. Then I remember why everyone is up here. Stella's only dressed in my robe—a robe that is practically falling off her perfect body that belongs only to me.

A seething anger full of possessiveness engulfs me. I spin around to see her in the white robe again, looking even more enticing, and I want to destroy that thing. "What the fuck are you doing out of the room in that thing?" If I didn't have my family standing around, I'd rip it right off of her body just to prove a damn point.

"What the fuck do you care?" she snaps, snatching the luggage from the ground and turning on her bare feet.

"We'll be in here," Grace says, sneering at me before following Stella and slamming the bedroom door.

"Oh, wow, Damiano. You have your hands full." My mother shakes her head at me, smiling so damn wide. I tilt my body back to my bedroom door, wanting to go in there and straighten her ass out. My mother grabs my bicep. "How about you go talk to your father while I check on your bride?"

Gabe steps in front of me and says, "Your mother has a point, Dame." I know he does because I'm not in the right frame of mind to do anything but teach my wife what happens if she ever wears another man's clothes again. Why the fuck does that bother me?

"Fine." I need a fucking drink or ten right now.

"Gabe, keep him from drinking too much." Did I say that aloud?

He nods to her. "Yes, ma'am."

I'm having a motherfucking breakdown. What is this woman doing to me? There is no way any woman has had this effect on me. *Ever.* I don't like it. She's nothing more than a beautiful face and a great distraction. I might not need sex, but it doesn't mean I don't want it. She's a convenient way to have it regularly. That's all. I won't let that look on her face get to me.

We enter my office and Gabe goes to my bar, pouring me a drink and handing it to me before standing guard over it. Quickly, I send it down my throat, letting it burn, but it's not enough. He gives me a warning look and fills the next one with a little less. He's fucking lucky my guns are tucked away, but if I get around my desk, my best friend might have a problem if he doesn't refill this motherfucker. I toss it back and set it on the table before taking a seat on my leather sofa with my feet kicked out.

My father has already taken the spot behind my desk like it's his. He must have been reading my damn mind about the guns, but I have others. "Son, explain what the hell has transpired and why the man who told me a month ago he would never marry has a wife."

"I had a point to prove."

"A point?"

"Yes, a bastard owed me money, then he had something I wanted. A fair deal. In fact, I'll be dealing with him soon. He's waiting for me in the special location, but since I promised a dinner, it will have to wait."

"You couldn't have just fucked the girl and sent her on her way?" My nostrils flare, and for the first time in a long time, I want to fight my father. Why was I pissed about my father's words?

Instead, I control myself because I'm not a ballsy teenager with temper issues. I'm the damn Don, and I do what the fuck I please. "Nope, I wanted to humiliate him and add insult to injury. Now I have a pretty, temporary toy until I grow tired of her. Will you be joining us for dinner?"

"I suppose your mother will definitely want to stay. I hope you know what you're doing."

"Don't I always?" I brush off his concerns because I have more important things to handle, like getting my hands on Stella's stepfamily and destroying them.

"You're in uncharted waters." The housekeeper knocks on the door to inform me that dinner is ready.

CHAPTER FIFTEEN

STELLA

y heart pounds as it aches while I try to process what just happened, although I'm not going to get a chance because Gracie follows me into the room as I toss the suitcase onto the bed. "Oh, Stella, you shouldn't listen to my brother."

I tug the zipper free and flip it open, sending several bras flying out of the luggage. I reach over and scoop them up before turning around to frown at my new sister. "Why? Gracie, aren't you the one who said your brother is a man of his word? Besides, he's right. I don't love him, and he doesn't love me." This time she frowns, and my heart hurts just a bit more than it did a moment ago, which I didn't think was possible.

Needing to break the tension, I ask, "What did you bring me? I know you have fabulous tastes, so please tell me you brought me something to make me feel at least semi-human right now." Her face immediately lights up, and that's the Gracie I met a few months ago.

"Of course I have." She whips out a gorgeous dinner dress that's white with pale blue dots, and it's perfect. "I also snatched up your things from the venue so I could get your sizes. More stuff will come soon, but luckily I was pretty accurate in my guess."

"Okay. I'm going to shower." I rush into the bathroom just as the door opens, thankfully avoiding whoever that is because I don't want to deal with anyone else before I can freshen up.

When I come out about ten minutes later, towels wrapped around me, I see the woman who I caught a glimpse of in the hallway, and she's sitting at the foot of the bed. "You must be the lovely Stella, my new daughter-in-law."

"Yes, I am."

"I put away your clothes and set your outfit on the credenza in the closet. You can change in there. We'll wait right here."

"Okay. Thank you." I step into the walk-in and close the door to his massive dressing room. I'm stunned at the magnificence of this place. As much as I hate to say it, I could enjoy being Damiano's paid-for wife, even if it's temporary.

Once I've slipped on the attire, I step out with the towels to hang in the bathroom. "I'll take these," Grace says.

"Come, sit with me," Mrs. Valentino says, taking my hands.

"This is a beautiful ring. Damiano went through a lot of trouble to pick out such a pretty ring for you."

"Yes, well. Appearances and all."

"Appearances? Do you think he attends functions?"

"No, but it's not like he can look bad giving me the garbage my last fiancé did after he just called him out on it."

His mother's brows flit upward, and her bright hazel eyes widen with curiosity with my slip. "Last fiancé?"

"Yes. Gracie didn't tell you?" I question, panic shooting through my body.

"I didn't know what Dame wanted me to say." Gracie shrugs like it's not an issue. I suppose it isn't for her to say since it's not her life that's affected by this mess. "Well, I'm going to see what's up with dinner. I'm getting hungry. Today's adventures built up my appetite."

"Don't think I've forgotten what your father and I walked in on, young lady."

"What? I've really got to go." She flees from the room like lightning.

I raise my brow, wondering what happened there.

"So this fiancé?"

"My stepfather sold me to someone else, and that piece of crap happened to owe your son money, so an even trade-off, I suppose." I wave my hands over my body.

She shakes her head and stands. "I'm going to slap my son. For what it's worth, I'm sorry that you're in this situation." She pulls me in for a hug and then excuses herself from the room. While she's gone, I finish getting prepared for dinner.

There's a knock at the door. "Come in."

"Are you sure?" he questions, pushing open the bedroom door cautiously, ducking his head.

"It's your room, Damiano," I answer while staring at him through the large mirror as I finish my hair.

"I didn't want you to toss some shit at my head," he confesses, closing the door behind him. The sheepish expression filled with guilt and contrition actually makes me feel sorry for him when it's my feelings that were hurt.

I shrug it off, trying to play the pain off since I don't have a right to be hurt. "Why? Like I told your sister—you didn't lie." His face hardens, but I can't read it. "I hope this is acceptable."

"Acceptable? You look fabulous. Fuck, it's going to be hard to eat my dinner when all I want is dessert." He licks his lips, and my treacherous body reacts. "Ready, Mrs. Valentino?"

"Yes, Mr. Valentino." He holds out his hand as a growl rips from his throat. I'd be concerned if lust wasn't shining from his eyes.

"Let's get dinner over with so I can send my parents and sister home."

"Is Gabriele not joining us?"

"He lives on the property."

"Oh."

"Why are you concerned about him?"

"It's just that he's been attached to your sister's hip all day."

"You're observant. Now, come along, Angel." He leads me to the dining room where the family is waiting for me.

Everyone is standing around with a drink in hand and claps as we enter.

"Congratulations to Mr. and Mrs. Damiano Valentino. May you have a long and fruitful marriage." He hands me a glass of wine and then takes one for himself. We all cheer and drink a sip before he takes the glass.

"Enough. Please, let us eat," Damiano grumbles. He takes the seat at the head of the table, seating me to his left. My stomach's twisted in knots, but I haven't managed to eat a single thing today. Despite the upset, my hunger pangs win out and I make it through dinner, but I mostly move my food around my plate.

His parents were charming the entire dinner, making conversation about their trip to Italy and Greece, taking the heavy out of the evening. "I believe it's time we take our leave."

"It's a pleasure to meet you, Stella. You're a treasure," my father-in-law says, taking my hand and kissing the back of it. A deep rumble comes from behind me. A slow smile spreads across his face.

"Paloma, perhaps you ladies would like to go shopping later this week. I'm certain there are many things Stella will need."

"Yes, I would love that, Firenze." She kisses her husband's cheek and then kisses mine. "My husband is right. I want to spoil my new daughter."

"Hey, I get to come too, right?"

"Of course, Gracie, dear. We'll make it a girls' trip."

"Thank you."

The moment they're gone, Damiano's eyes are focused on mine with dark, sensual intent. With a growl, he says,

"Enough with entertaining my family, Wife. It's time to entertain me." One moment I'm on my feet, and the next I'm upside down. He worships me the rest of the night, eating me for dessert as promised twice for good measure before slowly sinking into me and then roughly fucking me.

CHAPTER SIXTEEN

DAMIANO

A rapid knock on my bedroom door draws my attention. I wouldn't have heard it, but I haven't gone to bed since I can't take my eyes off my little wife who has been thoroughly fucked into a sex-induced coma. I slip on my boxers and go to the door.

I'd been so damn carried away with Stella's body that I forgot about the damn bastard in my cellar and Rocco's captives in the cabin. "Boss, I've been trying to get ahold of you for hours. I went up to the cabin. Vito's dead, and Rocco's gone along with the Joneses."

"Fuck."

I'm out of the room without waking my sleeping angel, and I can't ignore the damn bruises on her perfect body that I didn't leave there. When I get her father, he's going to pay for laying a hand on my woman and so much more.

"I want his fucking head on a platter, and then I'm going to destroy her family."

"What about our guest?"

"He's going to tell us what he knows before I destroy him for touching my wife."

"We'll get them all. I promise, Dame."

"Where's my father and Adriano?"

"They're downstairs waiting on you." We quickly make it down to my study where they're gathered.

"Marriage looks good on you, Son," my father teases, handing me a glass of whiskey. "Gabe told us about Vito. We know he was more than just a soldier; he was a good man and husband. Fucking Rocco is going to pay for his betrayal." I'd known Vito for ten years, and this is my failure to stay strong and rule with an iron fist like I always had.

"Yes, he is. I can't believe he'd risk it all for that slut."

"What do you mean?"

"Camille Jones. She was deep-throating his cock in my club, and I kicked her out about a month ago. He played me and said she drugged him. Tests said he was dosed with MDMA, so I bought his bit and gave the fucker a second chance, but the bastard was probably using. I didn't get the doctor to run a test to see if he's a habitual user. Hell, I don't know if there is a test for that shit."

"It doesn't matter now."

"I'm getting too damn soft. No more weakness." My mind goes to my wife who had turned me soft. Yes, this happened before I met her, but if I hadn't been so damn involved with her today, Vito wouldn't have been alone with Rocco in the middle of nowhere with no damn help.

My father's eyes narrow, but he doesn't say a word.

"Let's have a chat with your guest. I'm sure he's pissed his pants by now."

"And then some. Who's had eyes on him all day?"

"Benz and Michael," Adriano says.

"Okay, let's greet him." We all head to the basement, and Benz nods from the top of the stairwell.

"He's passed out. It reeks in there, just so you know. Like foul as fuck, so I've kept my distance."

"Where's Michael?"

"He went to take a break ten minutes ago. Should be back in five." He folds his nose, and I don't doubt him because the smell has already permeated the outer room. It's going to be a pain in the ass to clean up.

I push open the door, slamming it against the wall, but the fucker doesn't bother to lift his head, which hangs down to his chest. "Tommy, boy. Look at me, you asshole." I storm over to the bastard, a sinking feeling in my stomach. I lift his head, and the fucker's eyes have rolled back in his head.

"Merda."

"He's dead," my father sighs.

I check the fucker's pulse, and the prick is cold. "He's been dead for a while. Get Benz in here now." He comes into the room with his hand over his mouth. "What the fuck happened here?"

"What do you mean?" He starts gagging from the smell.

"This bastard is dead."

"Son of a bitch," he barks out. "Can we go in the hall?" The color on his face changes, and both my father and I move just in time to miss Benz vomiting. He's been in the family about two years, and I don't think he's ever seen a dead body before. He handles surveillance on the cameras.

"Get your shit together and meet us in the security room." I head in there with Gabe, Adriano, and my dad following me while Benz washes his face in the basin just ten feet from the cellar holding room.

"Fucking pussy."

"Pull up the feeds from the time Michael went on his supposed break." Gabe takes a seat and goes to work. It's not long before his taillights are seen leaving. "Break, my ass."

"Another traitor."

"Cue up the cell."

"Hello, Tommy Baker, it's good to see you again. I've waited a long time to see your fucking ugly mug." Michael walks up to him.

"Who are you?"

"Oh, you don't remember me? I was a lot younger then, and you weren't the big piece of shit you are now. Well, maybe you remember my sister…" Michael pulls out a picture and then Tommy flinches backward, nearly sending his chair backward. "I've wanted to end your miserable life for twenty years, but that's the boss's pleasure. God, I want to rip you limb from limb and enjoy it. You ruined her, destroyed her. Now I got you here, and I'm going to have a little fun before Mr. Valentino has his way with you for trying to steal his bride."

"Steal his bride? She was mine. He's a pussy."

"A pussy? He's the devil."

"The devil's going to be played. He hides his money in

plain sight, and he's so busy playing with her innocent little snatch that it's all going to be taken from him."

"That's not going to happen. None of his men will let that happen."

"His men? Ha. How do you think I knew who to ask? Why do you think Camille got close to that pretty little hummingbird? She's on so many radars. Now the wife is too. We have an inside man. He doesn't even know he's about to get robbed too."

"Liar."

"Those girls are going to end up just like your sister."

"Bastard," Michael roars, punching Tommy and sending his head snapping back, and that's when the footage shows Tommy slump over. Holy fuck.

He did something to Michael's sister twenty years ago, making him around twelve at the time. Just a kid when it happened. Fuck. No wonder Tommy had no idea who he was. I call Michael's cell. "Where the fuck are you?"

"I didn't mean to kill him, Boss." The sound of tears filled his throat, and for the first time in my life, I'm moved by it.

"I know you didn't, but I need you to calm the fuck down and tell me where you're going. What happened to your sister?"

"You can't ask me to calm down and then ask me what happened to her," he angrily chuckles. "Imagine the worst." I can't because I want to slice open the bag of worms in that room. He had every intention of destroying my sister and now Stella. I knew it. Never have a woman because they weaken you, make you vulnerable, and create...a soft spot.

"Come back. We have a lot of revenge to get, and I want you to get yours. Tommy's death was too easy and unfair. The fucker probably died from something else. That blow shouldn't have killed him, but I have others that need to pay for their transgressions, and we could use your help." I end the call and wait while Andriano loses his suit jacket and rolls up his sleeves to help clean up the mess in the room as he and Gabe's change into contamination suits.

"You look like a bitch," Adriano says.

"It smells, and I'm not getting that shit on my clothes."

"I've already dirtied these up bringing this asshole here earlier. I'll burn them." Adriano drops the fat fuck down on the drop cloth like a pile of bricks. "Hey, Boss. Maybe it's my fault this asshole died too quickly. I might have banged his head earlier, getting him into the trunk."

"He probably croaked because he was overweight, beaten, strapped to a chair, and worried. The man was one scare away from a heart attack," my father says. "Don't fret over bullshit. Get the job done because we have more pressing matters."

I pace the security area, and my mind goes to Stella. Always her. I can't decide if I'm better off without her. Once her enemies are gone, I know she'll be better without me. Yes, that's what will happen. After this is all over, I'll set her free. "Yes, my club is in danger."

"Do you think they have plans to attack it?" my father asks.

"You heard Tommy. They had an inside man. Rocco knows the club inside and out."

It takes twenty minutes for Michael to return, but once he does, he says, "I'm sorry I lost my cool."

"You should have told me."

"I didn't know it was him until he was in the cell. I didn't know his name, only his face."

"It's forgiven. Lie to me again, and I will have no mercy."

"Understood, Boss."

For the remainder of the evening, we go over everything Adriano found in the cabin as well as what we learned. There has been no trace of Rocco or the Joneses, but it's only been ten hours. It could be a while before we snuff them out of their hiding spot.

The events of the day have finally sunk in, and all I want to do is go upstairs and climb into my bed. Rubbing my hands over my face, I tell my men, "Everyone tuck it in for the night."

As everyone moves to exit, my father grips onto my shoulder. "Son, I'd like a word with you."

"What is it?" I answer, staying back.

His look is intense and sincere as concern mars it. "Stella's a good girl."

I nod. "An angel, and?"

"Exactly, so don't ruin her."

"I'm not." I'm saving her, and I'll give her a great life to live after she says goodbye to me. She'll find another man to worship her sexy body. The thought doesn't sit well with me, but neither does tainting her with my darkness.

CHAPTER SEVENTEEN

STELLA

I wake up, and Damiano isn't in our bed anymore. In fact, I haven't woken up with him in our bed for the past week. It's as if our wedding day and night were a fluke. A mere formality to prove we were married, consummating the marriage to make it valid, but nothing more. He hasn't even kissed my cheek when I enter the room. Nothing about our marriage seems the same as it did. That day was all for show.

I slide out of the bed, hating that I actually miss him. What's worse is I know he's at the club in the middle of the night and then comes home and sleeps elsewhere. Is it because he smells of some whore and he doesn't want me to know? That thought drives me nuts.

Thankfully I got my period last week, so there will be no consequences from our wedding night. Getting dressed and slipping on a cute pair of shorts with sandals and a tank top, I prepare for the Miami summer heat. With all our troubles gone, I can go out and enjoy life. Gracie, Mrs. Valentino, and I still haven't gone on our shopping trip, but since she returned, Mrs. Valentino has been insanely busy. Although given that I'm going to have a serious talk with my husband, we might not make it to that trip.

I exit our bedroom, and there is a guard outside my door, like there is every morning. They change it up, but I'm not sure if it's because they have a schedule or something, or because they like to keep me on my toes. However, I've had this tall, lanky guy who walks around in a leather jacket and jeans with a long braid. He's tatted on his neck and hands, but I don't pay attention to the details—only that he gives me the creeps. Almost like he doesn't fit in compared to the suits. It's stupid, but maybe it's because he's the oddball out. "Excuse me—Benz, is it?"

He gives me his attention. "Yes, Mrs. Valentino."

"It's Stella," I say, hoping to feel a little more at ease around him.

"Mrs. Valentino. How can I help you?" Damn it. There is no give with these people around here.

"I'm looking for Mr. Valentino," I say, wanting to see that dickhead husband of mine.

"He's in a meeting right now."

"Very well. Will you tell him I'm going for a walk and that I'll be back in an hour?"

"I can't let you do that, ma'am."

"What? Am I a prisoner in this home?" I question.

"It's the boss's orders." I toss him a dirty look and flip my ponytail as I stroll right past him and down the stairs.

"We'll see about that." I storm to his office, which I

haven't been inside of because the doors are always closed, and he never lets me look inside. "Damiano, I'd like to talk—" I push open the double wooden doors to see my husband with a gun to a man's head while his father, Gabriele, and two other men all stare at me.

"Leave."

"Sorry, Boss."

Benz takes my arm and pulls me from the room, and then I hear a noise that can only be a muffled gunshot a moment later. "Benz, don't ever put your hands on my wife again, or you'll be next." Damiano grabs me by the waist and flips me over his shoulder, carrying me upstairs in a rush.

"Wife, what was so urgent that you felt the need to barge into my office like that?" Panic washes over me. I can't ask for a divorce now. What if he tries to kill me next? I have no idea what he's capable of.

"Damn it, I knew it. Stella, stop the fucking tears. You're not going to put this on me. I told you to stay out of there, and I'm sure you were told not to interrupt me. Why can't you do what you're told?"

"I was told I can't go on walks," I finally confess, stomping my foot.

He fists my hair, pulling me close so that his lips are just an inch from mine. "No, you fucking can't. Soon, though, you'll be free to do whatever you want."

"What does that mean?"

"When I find your stepfather, stepsister, and that bastard Rocco who helped them escape, I'll give you a divorce. You can have a happy life with all the damn strolls your heart desires. So, for now, you behave and be a good little wife." I stared at him, stunned, confused, brows twisting.

The only word that I can form is, "Okay."

He releases me roughly, seemingly annoyed with my response. "I have to shower and then go back to work."

"Work," I scoff, taking a seat on the bed. His shoulders tense up and he stops walking, turning to look at me. I expect a cold glare, but the look of disappointment is worse.

He turns back around and enters the bathroom, closing the door without a word. My head and heart are confused, even after this short time.

As much as I need space from him, I also need answers. There's nothing for me to do outside the room anyway, so I sit on the bed and wait. He doesn't keep me in suspense for long.

With a dark sneer, he says, "I'm surprised you're still there."

"Why? You act as though I have anything else to do."

"Yes, my home is so boring, Angel." He rolls his eyes.

"Listen, Mr. Valentino. Why don't we just get this over with now? You can file for divorce already. It's not like it matters to you anyway. I appreciate you stopping that horrible marriage and introducing me to the world of hot sex, but since those are both over, I can go on my merry way and find a real life and husband somewhere else."

He's on me in a second, eyes darkened, hand on my throat with enough force to hold me in place but not completely cutting off my air. "You're my wife until I say so, and you will not dare mention another man in my bed ever again."

How dare he? It's like a slap in the face to be left in limbo. "Why? You don't touch me. You don't want me after you find them, so what does it matter?"

"You want me to touch you, Wife? You want me to fuck you?" I bite down on my lip, damn near drawing blood. He tugs my lip free from my teeth's grip.

"Don't bite what's mine, Amore." His mouth crashes down on mine, roughly taking my breath away.

I rip my lips away and hiss, "I'm not yours."

Damiano's hand on my throat tightens while the other grips my wrist, lifting my hand up to my face. "This says otherwise." The shiny diamond ring is nothing but a mockery to me.

Staring into his stormy gray eyes, I remind him of his words. "It's temporary."

"Keep pushing me, Angel." He pins me to the bed with his firm body holding me down.

"What are you going to do? Show me how much you're just like the animals you saved me from?"

"No, I'm going to give you just what you want," he groans, dropping his lips to mine again and brutally kissing my lips, and I can't fight the longing. My thighs easily part, wanting and craving his touch. I give in so easily and he takes what he wants, making me come apart as he buries his massive cock in me until we're both crying out in pleasure.

The second we're both sated, he climbs off me, forgets all the tender passion, and dresses, leaving me naked and alone.

CHAPTER EIGHTEEN

DAMIANO

She's sitting in the kitchen with a cup of orange juice, not even coffee, and I fight the urge to switch it for her. There's just something so damn innocent about her that drives me insane. My sweet little wife turns me on with everything she does, but she's only eighteen.

"No coffee?"

"I don't know where it's at."

"You didn't ask the chef to make it for you?" She blushes, and a hint of jealousy fills me. Is she interested in my younger chef?

"Um, he's a chef. Besides, I didn't want to impose." Damn. What kind of life did she have with her stepfather? That piece of shit probably limited her meals or made her ask for permission. Am I any better? She can't do shit without my say, but it's not for the same reason.

"This is your home," I tell her, wanting to be different than Jones.

"For now," she reminds me. Fuck. Eating my own words burns in my gut. A part of me wishes I'd cut my tongue out for slipping up like that.

My hand cups her chin. "Don't spread that around to everyone. I'd hate for anyone to treat you with a lack of respect." She cocks her brow and purses her lips, dipping her eyes to where my hand is.

Releasing my grip, I turn around and start the coffee, ignoring the pointed reference that I don't treat her with respect. She gets more respect out of me than anyone else. The way she talks back would have cost her life. Once the pot is brewing, I face her and say, "My mother would like you to join her and Gracie to go shopping today."

"Oh, really?" Stella's eyes widened. "I can go?"

"Yes, but you'll be under guard the entire time, so don't try anything stupid." She twists her lips, giving me a confused frown. "What do you have to say now?"

"Nothing."

"Don't lie to me."

"No, I don't have anything to say to you, Mr. Valentino. I'm cool. It will be good to see your sister again. Now, I appreciate the release off house arrest."

"It's for your safety, Stella."

"I get it. It's you being a prick about it. What did you think I'd do that would be so stupid? I lived with a man who hadn't let me leave the house in four years. I'm not tripping about a few months."

I lose the distance between us and ask in disbelief, "Four years?"

"Yes, so you can see how being cooped up can feel a bit overwhelming."

"I'm sorry." She snaps her head back, surprised by my apology. Hell, so am I. Frankly, I can't remember the last time I ever said sorry for a damn thing.

"Here's my card."

"Oh, no. Are you sure you trust me with this? You might be broke by the time I get back," she warns me with a devious smile that cracks something deep inside my chest.

"Wife, you could spend to your heart's content and still not bankrupt us. Trust me—my mother has given my father a run for his money." She giggles, and I pull her into my arms. "Have some fun. We'll have dinner together tonight, and you can maybe try something on for me." I wink, kiss her forehead, and then release her. The stunned look on her face matches the one on mine. Fuck—what am I doing? This isn't what I signed up for. Lust. I married her to slake the lust she brings out in me. That's all. Temporary, pleasurable, and that's it.

I rush out of the kitchen, forgetting all about my coffee, and adjust my aching cock. What am I going to do about this feeling in my chest?

CHAPTER NINETEEN

STELLA

Hanging out with Gracie and Mrs. Valentino was incredible as we shopped, ate lunch, and gossiped for hours, but all I could think about was getting home to Damiano and our special dinner.

He'd been different this morning when I confessed my imprisonment. The way he held me and the intense look in his beautiful, stormy gray eyes felt like we had a breakthrough.

I picked out the perfect dress for dinner tonight. I skipped up to our bedroom with my purchases, or rather, Adriano helped me. "Goodness, what did you do, buy out the store?"

"Come on, you're built like a building. Is it really that heavy? I can take them from you."

"Ha. The boss man would have my neck."

"Do you know when he'll be back?"

"He's in his office, but you know you can't interrupt him."

"Yep. Learned my lesson, unless there's a bitch in there." I give him a side eye.

"You don't have to worry about that, Mrs. Valentino."

"Says you, but he owns a club called Body Count and there are half-naked women dancing around there, and he's very comfortable up in that suite of his. He has tons of women up there."

"What? Who told you that bullshit lie? If I were you, I'd never say that in front of Mr. Valentino. He wouldn't take it too kindly. That's for business and friends only."

"Yes, but my stepsister was up there, so there's no accounting for taste."

"That was a safety precaution, and Gracie got an earful for that, I'm sure." He nods and chuckles. "By more than the boss man."

"Thanks." We stop at the bedroom and I open the door, entering first. Adriano sets the bags on the floor near the door and then says, "If you need anything, I'm outside here until there's a need for a switch."

"Thank you again."

"No problem, Mrs. Valentino." He nods and steps out of the room, closing the door behind him.

I take a moment to sit on the bed without saying a word and let out a hard breath. It's been on my mind since that night, but I refuse to bring it up because there is nothing that will change the past. So what did he mean by it? Did she put her hands on him? That's possible. She could have flirted with him, and he brushed it off like the jerk at the bar did with me. I didn't welcome it, but it happened anyway and there wasn't a way to stop it.

A knock shakes me out of my thoughts. "Yes?"

"Mrs. Valentino?"

"Come in, Adriano."

He opens the door and peeks in. "Mr. Valentino would like to have an early dinner since he needs to be at the club in two hours. Please be ready in an hour."

"Okay. Thank you." He closes the door, and I look for the sexy dress I plan to wear and hang it up. If he doesn't intend on staying home with me, it's pointless to wear. Grabbing a cute dress, I slide it from the closet and wash up in the shower, leaving my hair pinned up since I don't have time to dry it.

When I finish preparing for my evening with my husband, I'm a ball of nerves. This could totally go sideways. Damiano and I haven't said or done much together since we've married but fight or have sex.

Since I'm ready early, I leave my room, only to run directly into my husband's broad chest. "Whoa," Damiano says, catching me before I fall back.

"Sorry, I thought we'd meet downstairs."

"We are. I wanted to clean up. Stella, you look beautiful."

"Thank you."

He releases me and says, "I'll be ready shortly. Do you want to wait in our room, or downstairs?"

"I'll be in the library."

"Very well, Stella." He kisses my cheek and passes by to go into the bedroom.

Benz is on the steps waiting for me. "Mrs. Valentino," he mutters an obligatory greeting.

"Benz. I'll be in the library. You don't need to escort me there."

"I do."

"Okay—if you enjoy being a glorified babysitter." I huff my way down the marble staircase. The mansion is truly gorgeous. If my life had been different, if Damiano had feelings for me, I could absolutely fall in love with this magnificent home. Instead, it feels like a luxurious cage.

When I open the library doors, I get an icky feeling that Benz is going to follow me inside. It's so weird that I didn't get a strange vibe when Adriano, the giant tank, brought the clothes into the bedroom, but the lean Benz follows me anywhere and I want to jump out of my skin. Would it be wrong to mention it to Damiano? Probably. He's a mobster—"the" mobster. He's likely either to tell me I'm paranoid or take his man out back and put a bullet in his head because I'm being irrational.

"You don't need to be in the room with me. I'm perfectly safe inside the library unless I manage a paper cut, and I'm pretty sure Damiano already told you that you weren't allowed to touch me." He scoffs and closes the door on his way out. "Prick."

I pace the library, looking for something of interest, but my nerves are frayed. Picking up a nicely bound edition of Mary Shelley's *Frankenstein*, I sit down on a high winged-back chair and rest my feet on the matching ottoman. With a sigh, I begin the classic and fall in love with the first few chapters before my eyes grow heavy.

I don't know what time it is when I startle awake, but Damiano enters our bedroom. "I didn't mean to wake you, sleeping beauty."

"Well, it's hard to eat dinner in my sleep."

"I'm afraid it's well past dinner, but we can go down to the kitchen and I'll fix you breakfast."

"Breakfast?" I gasp. "How did I get in here? Did one of your men carry me?"

"Not unless they wanted to lose their hands." That brings an internal burst of joy to my chest. "I went to check on you for dinner, but you were asleep. I didn't want to wake you, so I carried you to bed and then I went to the club early."

And there goes all happiness, joy dashed. "Oh. No, I don't need breakfast. I'd rather just go back to bed."

"Good. I'm tired." He slides under the covers and pulls me into his arms, holding me tightly as if somehow there's nothing wrong with what happened tonight. As much as I want to cry, I won't. You can't make someone love you.

"Goodnight, or morning, Damiano."

"Goodnight, my wife," he sighs sleepily.

"For now," I whisper, voice cracking as my hopes for us fade away.

CHAPTER TWENTY

DAMIANO

It's been a month since they disappeared, but there have also been no more attacks on my businesses either. The last one had been the night we were supposed to have dinner together. I thought it had been a blessing that she'd fallen asleep because I would have disappointed her by canceling our dinner and rushing out of the house, but hearing her voice crack did something to me. No, I wasn't planning on keeping her forever, but I don't know if I'll ever be able to let her go.

The more I deny my feelings for her, the more I'm faced with the fact that death will be the only way I'll leave her. Still, I haven't forgotten what I overheard between her and Benz. She thought I walked straight into the bathroom, but I waited like a needy damn husband before she went down the stairs. There's a tension between them, and not a sexual one—at least not on her end. She doesn't like him. I should be worried because Stella's been around enough unscrupulous people to trust her gut. Why hasn't she told me about it? Maybe because I haven't given her enough attention or trust. Either way, Benz needs to be looked into.

I'm on the phone to my second, needing to discuss this issue right away. "Gabe, meet me in my office now."

"I'm on my way, Dame," he says. I end the call and turn on the cameras to the library where Stella's currently reading *Dracula*. I haven't picked up those books in years, but she seems intrigued. After my meeting with him, I'm going to take her out for a nice stroll, maybe even seduce my sexy wife under the full moon tonight. My dick hardens like it always does for her, but it's not the proper time, so I adjust myself and calm down.

"You summoned me?" Gabe asked, stepping inside and closing the door.

"Yes. Who is watching Stella right now?"

"Benz is."

A deep rumble comes from my chest. "That's what I thought. I want you to dig into his background a little more." I should move him, but I know he wouldn't do anything with everyone in the house watching because it would mean a death sentence. He'd have to wait where he could escape.

He twists his lip up. "How did he come recommended to us?"

"He was working for one of the twins and helped at the club until we had that incident with the Irish," I informed Gabe why I felt Benz had earned my respect. His help had protected more than just my club, but he saved Sasha and several of the workers who had nearly been killed.

"Oh, yeah. He killed three of the Irish that day. How was he such a bitch in the basement with Baker?" Truthfully the smell was a bit much to take even for me, but we were used to death so he should have been used to it too.

"I don't know, but I get the feeling Stella doesn't like him."

"Have you asked her?" he questioned, raising his naturally perfectly shaped brows up at me. He's lucky we're fucking close or I'd have to pop him in the mouth.

"No."

"You know, communication works with your wife."

I narrowed my eyes at him. "What would you know about a wife? Are you planning on talking about my sister with me?"

"What?" He pales.

"Don't fucking lie to me, Gabriele. We've been friends way too long for you to bullshit me."

"There's nothing going on between us... yet." He rubs his hands together, cracking his knuckles.

"But..."

"I'm in love with her, and I haven't figured out if you planned on killing me for it." His eyes meet mine, waiting for my blessing or refusal.

"If there was ever a man I'd want to marry my sister, it would be you, but have you considered what my father would say?"

"He's already asked when I'm going to stop letting Gracie walk all over me, and when I'll stand up and ask for your permission. So, as my oldest friend, do I have permission to marry your sister?"

I chuckle at the pussy because my sister's adorable, but if I know anything, she's going to be like my mother and she's going to rule him. "You don't need my permission, but you have my blessing."

He stands and shakes my hand. "Thank you. So what do you want me to do about Benz?"

"I want all of his past. There's something bothering me, and I want it now. I wish I'd dug deeper before."

"He had more than proven himself before. If anything, he so far he's still the man. All we have is Stella's discomfort."

"For me that's good enough," I say.

"Good." He stands and leaves. Now, it's time to make my wife a lot more comfortable. I rake my tongue over my teeth, aching to take a bite out of her tempting pulse.

CHAPTER TWENTY-ONE

STELLA

I feel Damiano the moment he enters the library, even though I can't see him yet. The closer he gets, the quicker my heart speeds up. For the past week, he's been stealing visits into the library and making small talk. Each time, I get the sense that he wants more of me, desire pulling us closer and pushing us apart. Or rather, his men pulling him away. Something is always sending him from the room. I want to throw myself into his arms, but I'm afraid of his rejection.

"How's the book?" Damiano says, voice smooth, drawing a tremble throughout my body. Honestly, I couldn't tell him because the second I sat in the chair, I daydreamed he'd sneak into the library, take the book from my hand, toss it aside, lift up my skirt, and eat my pussy.

I tilt my head to look up at him as he places his hand on the back of the chair. "Good. Have you read it before?"

He moves to the ottoman, lifting my feet and setting them onto his thighs. "Yes, but it's been ten plus years."

"Wow, does someone come in here and dust everything?" I tease. Of course there's a full household staff.

"With as much as you read, there doesn't need to be as much dusting."

"Well, I've got to keep myself busy," I say, clapping my hand to my mouth to shut it when I see him frown. "Sorry. We were actually having a polite conversation."

"No. I've been leaving you all by yourself." His hand rubs my ankle, and a moan falls from my lips as my head rolls back on the chair. His hand slowly moves higher.

"My dark prince," I moan.

"Yes, my dear Mina?" Hearing him call me Dracula's greatest love goes straight to my heart. He tosses the book aside, sliding his hand up until my dress is at my waist.

Our eyes meet, and I see the hunger that matches my own. "I'm famished," he growls. My panties are pushed to the side with his adept fingers.

Whimpers fall from my lips and then his heated breath lands on my inner thigh, methodically teasing me. "Damiano, I need…" I plead, unsure of what I'm asking for.

"I know, baby. You need to come on my tongue before I fill that tiny little slit."

"Please eat me up."

"I love to hear you beg for it," he growls before his tongue swipes across my seam. He eats me out until I'm screaming his name.

"I need you inside me."

"Good girl." I drag him up to kiss me, tasting myself on his tongue while he frees himself from his slacks. My sensitive hole vibrates as he runs the bulbous tip up and down, edging my wet lips. "Oh my God."

He lifts me off the chair and takes me onto his lap. "Ride me." Slowly he slides me down his thick rod. "Yes, oh, yes." I drop my head onto his shoulder.

One hand lands on my ass, squeezing it tightly while the other cuffs the back of my neck, bringing my mouth to his. "Mine." His words drive me on. I ride my husband wildly, coming fast and hard, and then I feel him give me every drop of his release, roaring his seed into me as if he's forgotten that we'll soon be a thing of the past.

I let my head fall onto his broad shoulder so he can't see what the thought does to me.

"Stella, I didn't come in here to get between your thighs again."

"Well, it would seem like you did."

"I'm not going to say being buried deep inside your tight cunt doesn't feel incredible, but I thought we'd take a stroll outside today."

"What?" I gasp, leaning my head back to look at him.

"Would you like to stroll around the grounds with me?"

"I'd love it." I hop off his lap.

"Whoa, beautiful. Careful."

"Sorry." I bend down and kiss his penis.

"It's okay. You can kiss my cock anytime you want to say sorry."

I swat his arm and shake my head. "When are we going?" I ask as I move my panties back in place.

"The second we adjust our clothes." He fixes himself and then takes my hand.

"I need to use the bathroom first."

"Lead the way." We wash up, and then he takes me to the large back garden where all the fun outdoor activities are.

"How come I can't ever come out here?"

"Without me? It's too dangerous. Right now, my men have drones and cameras to survey any threats. As much as the land is protected, Rocco knows his way around the estate."

"But right now we're out here."

"The compound is on complete lockdown for this. Besides, we have a lead on his movements."

"Okay. Sorry. I don't mean to pester."

"Don't apologize. We can't stay outside for too long, though." We take a trail along the house until we reach an open garden area, but it's extremely hot outside today. As much as I love walking with him, I'm fighting the heat. I don't want to complain, but I'm about to faint.

"Stella, what's wrong?"

"Nothing."

"Don't lie to me. I hate liars." Suddenly his voice is icy cold.

"It's hot out here, if you can't tell by my suddenly cherry-red face."

"Well, you wanted to come out in ninety-five-degree heat after we just screwed like animals."

"I didn't know what the temp was. It's not like I have access to the outside temps," I remind him.

"Shit, I forgot." He frowns. He takes my hand and

kisses it before wiping the sweat off my forehead. "We can go for a swim in the pool."

"It's okay. We can cut this short. It looks like one of your minions is about to summon you." He turns and scowls as Benz comes scurrying toward us. God, I hate that man for some strange reason.

"It better be important because my wife and I are spending some quality time together. Can it wait?"

"It can't."

"I'll just take a shower. I'm tired anyway." I walk right past him into the house, ignoring all the safety protocols because I don't give a fuck anymore.

After my icy cold shower, Gracie stops by with a big old grin. "Hey, sis. What are you up to today?"

"Not a damn thing. I'm surprised you're allowed out of the house. Isn't it so dangerous right now?"

"Nope. I think my brother uses that excuse so you can stay put and his goons can keep an eye on you. I say we should head back to my house or do something else." Immediately, I'm filled with jealousy.

"What do you want to do?"

"We can go to the movies or go shopping."

I have an idea that flits through my head. "How about we watch a movie at your house, and then we head to his club later tonight?"

"I love it, but we'll have to be slick about it. As long as we use my dad as our backup for your security, then Damiano's guard dogs won't say shit."

"Yay. I need to get out of this house." We head to her house, but not before I get the dress I've been dying to wear for my temporary husband.

"Where are you headed, Mrs. Valentino?" Nico asks.

"We're going to watch a movie at Gracie's."

"I'll escort you there, but you can't leave without the elder Mr. Valentino's guards."

"I totally understand."

CHAPTER TWENTY-TWO

DAMIANO

"You're going to tell me what you know, or you're not going to make it out of here." Another bloody night of interrogation with an associate of Jones's. Frankly, I'm tired of it. No one has been any the wiser that I've wiped out half his acquaintances because the pussy would rather have everyone he knows go down than face me.

"I don't know anything, Mr. Valentino," Greg Pace stammers, eyes glossy and wide from the line of blow he did in my club when he didn't think we were watching. That only sets me off more. Turning my establishment into a cesspool of drugs isn't acceptable. The strip club is his usual haunt, but we dragged him over here and he needed a hit before he graced me with his overly cologne-wearing presence.

"That's bullshit, and we all know it. You worked for

that piece of shit, and you were screwing his daughter before they disappeared." He gasps. "Yes, we know a lot more than you think we do. So please, do keep playing games with me."

"I swear, I haven't spoken to her in two weeks." Two weeks? She's been on the run for much longer than that. So, she's heading back to her contacts and using them. We're closer to finding them, and then I'll have to find another reason to keep my wife close to my side. A plan already forms in my head, one I was subconsciously doing and will continue to do every time I get my hands on her delectable ass.

"Well, then, you do have much to tell me."

Adriano's phone goes off, and he answers it. He frowns, and I glare at him. "I told you I didn't want any interruptions, so it better be important."

"Boss, we have a situation. Your wife is in the club."

"What the fuck did you say?" Did I just hear him correctly?

"She's here and coming this way, according to Nico. He almost didn't let her in, but he didn't want to touch her."

"Well, he was wise about that." I want to smash this fucker's face in. I turn to my guest who now has seconds to give me what I want. "Where is she? Now. That's all the time you have left."

"She was with some dude in West Palm Beach. I gave her money after a quickie. She said she'd call me if she needs me for anything else."

"You have his phone?" I ask. It has been powered off,

but we are going to use it to our advantage to locate our enemies and flush them out after I take out the trash. This piece of shit in front of me isn't any better than the other scum. What he doesn't know is that I'm aware of his help on the arson of my building. It seems Rocco wasn't just working with Baker to rob me; he was trying to take down my empire in subtle ways. One warehouse at a time.

"Good."

A knock at the door reminds me that my little wife, who deserves an ass-spanking, has just arrived.

"We'll continue this in a moment." I step away from my guest and walk to the door, but the door is slightly ajar and I see my sweet angel dressed like sin—pure lust wrapped up in guilty pleasure, covered in nothing but fuck-me material. "What the fuck are you wearing, and what are you doing here?"

"I'm wearing a dress, and why is it a big deal that I'm at your club, Husband?" She looks around me as if she's trying to find something. I'm seething, wanting to shut this motherfucker down right now. How many dicks were eyeing my wife?

I call into the room and say, "Gabe, I want footage from the moment she walked in until the moment we got her in here."

"You want to know what I'm doing in here, Wife?" I open the door to my office where Camille's lover is tied up, waiting for my return.

"Take him somewhere more private. We'll have to finish this later. My wife seems to think showing everyone in this club what belongs to me is appropriate." I don't miss that the tied-up bastard's eyes linger on my wife's body. Seething, I've added a mental note to spice up his torture. I'll ask Adriano if we have cattle prods or if we can get them somewhere at this late hour.

"No one comes up here," I warn my staff.

"Yes, Boss," Adriano says.

Turning to my wife, I cuff her bicep and drag her off to the VIP lounge. "You want to come in here dressed in a slip of a piece of cloth for what? To get some asshole to notice you?"

"You certainly did." I want to spank that ass of hers.

"Yeah, I did. Bend over," I snarl, tossing her onto the same seat I had her on the first time she came into the club.

"Why?" she asks, but I push her shoulders down and she's forced onto all fours.

"Don't fucking argue with me. Don't question me, Stella. You are my wife, and you come in here while I'm working, distracting me with your pussy practically on display for all the guys in the club to see." I run my finger over her slit that's already wet. She might be putting up an attitude, but her little cunt is soaked with need.

"You're mine, and showing off this cunt isn't smart because I'll fucking kill every little dick out there for trying to touch you. Do you understand me?"

"I'm only yours for a little while longer."

"Until we're done, you're mine," I snapped, spanking her ass. She cries out.

"Go ahead, Angel. No one can hear your cries up here. Pop that ass back and take your spanking." Her reddened cheeks stiffen my dick to pure stone, so I free my cock before I come in my pants. I line my tip at her sopping wet hole and push my way in as I fist her hair.

"Damiano," she screams as I bottom out inside her tight cunt.

"That's right. Say my name. Shout that motherfucker as I fuck this tight hole. I own this pussy, Stella." I grab the front of her dress and tug down the material, holding her massive breasts in my palms. If I wasn't so fucking possessive about people seeing her naked, I'd put her tits on the glass. Fuck, I'm so damn close.

"I love the way you take this big dick. Your wet hole is so tight around me, begging for it."

"Yes, Dame."

"Come, Stella. Come." My thumb reaches down and presses her clit, and she squirts on the leather. Fuck, that sends me over the edge and I fill her up, shooting deep inside her. I pull out and she scrambles to adjust herself, face flush. She's too sexy to stay at the club tonight. Everything about her screams delectable, including the just-been-smashed look. I can't keep her by my side since I have business to handle, so my temper grows.

As she fixes herself, I stare, wanting another round, but there are things to do so I lead her back to my office where I take a spare suit blazer from my coat closet and cover her body. I say, "Now it's time for you to go home."

"Are you serious?" she hisses.

"Of course I am." I adjust my suit and then summon Adriano. "Take Mrs. Valentino home and make sure that she doesn't leave the estate. I have matters to attend to." There's still the mess we made on the seats, which I'll personally clean up because I don't want anyone touching my wife's release.

"Forgive me for forgetting my place, Mr. Valentino." She follows Adriano out of the club, and I know I screwed up, but what could I do? Business has to carry on.

CHAPTER TWENTY-THREE

STELLA

Damiano never came home last night. I was given a message by the housekeeper, of all people, that said the boss had important business and wouldn't be back for a couple of days. Interesting. None of my usual guards were there, but I still managed to sneak out to my in-laws' the next day because I had to get away. After what happened, I have a feeling everything is coming to an end. An end I don't want to face head on.

"It's nice to have you over, but it's clear you don't want to be here." Gracie can read how miserable I am, even though I've tried to keep a smile on my face.

"No, it's not that, Gracie. You're wonderful and perfect. It's just—"

"My brother is an asshole." Her face hardens, and she clenches her fists at her sides. When she's angry, she's like an adorable kitten.

"Girl, I thought he'd be my saving grace, but…" I break down crying, my heart tearing to pieces. "I'm nothing but his toy that he's waiting to dispose of."

"He cares about you," she says.

"Not enough, and not in the right way. This marriage is temporary and only until he finds my stepfather, but we don't even know if he's alive or where he's hiding. It could be days, or years. Then, he's going to end it like he promised before he sent me home from the club yesterday. I can't deal with it anymore. I deserve better."

She cradles me in her arms and whispers in my ear, "You do, you do." We sit like that for a moment when she says, "How about I help you escape?"

I pull away and stare at her, wondering if she's playing some game with me. "You would do that?"

She stands and paces. "He may be my brother, but you're also my sister, and he doesn't realize what he's losing. Maybe it will teach him a lesson in love."

I can only hope, but the man is set in his ways. "How can we do this?"

The first thing we plan on is maneuvering around his guards. With the amount of people coming and going less and less, I have a few guys not quite on me. Still, Gracie is almost just as guarded, but she has her parents on her side, and they're not as strict as Damiano. I head home and pack while she makes a few private shopping trips. My heart aches as I sit on our bed, thinking about never seeing my handsome, insanely frustrating husband again. My stomach turns and I rush off to our bathroom, violently retching out my lunch.

It's been three days since I left Damiano, and I find myself in a nicer motel than expected. Gracie did a great job. The money she gave me should last until I find a job nearby. Luckily, I still have my state ID and birth certificate with my maiden name and can use that to reapply for things once I reach a different state. The weather isn't as bad in Tennessee this time of year, so maybe I will end up in Nashville and far away from my soon-to-be ex-husband. Grace even managed to get me a disposable phone, so I don't have any traces of my past life. All I need to do is find a way to lay low for another week; maybe Damiano won't notice, and then I'll travel farther than Tallahassee.

I rest my head on the pillow, needing some relief from the past twenty-four hours. Running hadn't been easy physically or mentally, and now that it's done, maybe the ache in my chest can settle.

I wake up and take off running to the bathroom, losing everything in my stomach. Dropping back onto my haunches, I sit there to catch my breath. Damn it. I thought this feeling would go away after I left him, but it hasn't. Could it be that I'm coming down with something? Or could I be…pregnant? There is a huge possibility on that front. Damiano hasn't been careful at all, despite his protests about our short marriage arrangement.

Cleaning myself up, I get dressed and head out to the local pharmacy. It's a short walk, but even still, I have my hair tied up in a ponytail and covered up with a baseball cap.

With my shifty behavior in the store, I garner some

attention from the clerks. I'm sure they think I'm going to steal something, but I quickly put what I need in the basket, including a few snacks to keep me locked up in the motel for the night.

"Find everything all right, miss?"

"Yes," I answer, trying to avoid the cameras, just in case Damiano had someone scanning facial recognition databases or some crazy shit like that. Not that I'm sure he's looking too hard for me. After all, he did want to get rid of me soon.

When she sees what is in my basket, a sense of dawning comes over her face, a motherly look of concern as well. "I'm sure everything will be fine."

"Thanks. You never know if it's a stomach bug or something, right?" I say, trying to be as nonchalant as possible.

"Of course." She looks at my bare finger, and the sympathy is there again. She has no idea that I've tucked that five-carat bad boy away, waiting for the right time to pawn it. If I'm having his baby, I may need the money.

I pull out the money from my purse and pay for the purchases, quickly returning to the motel. As anxious as I was to get the test, suddenly I'm afraid to take it. A dread fills me. If I am expecting, doesn't he have the right to know his child? Would he want to? What would he do to me if he finds out I kept his child from him?

Stress makes my stomach roll several times, so I take the crackers I bought and snack on them. They ease my tummy a little, but only just.

Finally, my bladder makes the courageous decision for me. "Well, it's now or never." I head into the bathroom and open the packets, taking the motel's disposable cups and catching my sample. After two grueling minutes, I look and see that I'm not sick. Damiano stole my heart and left his baby.

Why can't he just want me? I gave him my heart and loved him foolishly. It was naïve to think he was my hero, my dark prince, because I was so wrong. Tears fall until I pass out in bed.

CHAPTER TWENTY-FOUR

DAMIANO

We've just laid eyes on Rocco after a full twenty-four hours of running down the leads from Miami to West Palm Beach and are about to nab him when Benz calls. "What is it?"

"Someone tried to set Body Count ablaze, but they failed." Yes, the place is wired tight to stop people getting in unless you're skilled.

"What?" I roar.

"The police and fire department are here, looking for you." Fuck. I don't have time for this bullshit. I want to get home to my wife and end everyone threatening her, including my empty threats.

"I'm on my way." I end the call.

I look over at Adriano and Michael. "Someone keep tabs on him. Never let him out of your sight. Any movements that lead to Jones, alert me." I explain about the club and drive off in a flash with Gabe.

Body Count. I should be thinking about the club, but my mind goes straight to my wife and what happened there. The look on her face had been one of pure hurt, and I put it there.

I arrive at Body Count and find that the scene is mostly cleared up, but there is caution tape around the building and front doorframe, and glass windows are boarded up. Quickly, I call the inspector. "Too busy to answer my calls?"

"Yes, it seems your places are very popular."

"What the fuck does that mean?" I snarl, not in the mood for cryptic games from the unhelpful city worker.

"Your other facility on the Miami Beach Marina has just been torched."

"Fucking son of a bitch." Heads are going to roll. "What are you doing about this?"

"Putting them out, Mr. Valentino. Where were you this evening?"

"Looking for answers out of town. Now, if you'll excuse me, I have to check on my wife to ensure her safety." I end the call and fly fast down the road to my estate. I've called Benz and see if he's in the house to check on Stella, but he doesn't answer.

"Something's not right. That asshole Benz isn't answering. Did we get the information on him?"

"Not yet. In fact, I have less information on his past, like his name isn't Anthony Benzino like he said. The real Anthony Benzino supposedly was killed in a gun battle three years ago."

"What?"

"Although there could be another."

"Check Benzino's relatives and friends." He continues to dig, and I wish I hadn't let that bit slip in the past two days, but there were too many fucking problems to push and Gabe's the only one I trust.

"Shit, it's going to take a while longer," Gabe grumbles. A sick, twisted feeling in my gut filled with dread takes over. All I can think about is that something is wrong where Stella's concerned. I don't know why I didn't give her a cell phone. Hell, I know exactly why. Because it would mean I'd have a chance to call her for no damn reason, a way for her to find an escape to the outside world and me.

I call my staff at the estate and ask about my wife. "Sir, we believe she is at your parents'. She hasn't been here since yesterday. Benz dropped her off yesterday." I ended the call because they were useless to me now.

"We're going to my parents'." I speed off in their direction, switching off the last five minutes in the opposite road. Fuck, I'm so damn close. When I pull into the driveway, I barely put it into park before I'm out of the SUV and rounding the front of it. Taking the stairs two at a time, I push past my parents' guards and into the house.

"Where is she?" I roar, tearing through my parents' home. When her guards said she wasn't home yet, I nearly lost my already insane mind. Our delicious fuck at the club had been one that pushed me over the edge. I want more and I need her to stay, even if it taints everything I have lived with inside my deranged head and heart.

"Calm down, Son. Who are you looking for?" my father asks, stepping in front of me as I run up the stairs where I know she's likely to be.

"Who the fuck else? My wife." I shrug his arm off me.

"She's not here," the hardened voice of my sister comes from behind me. I spin around, flying down the steps in a rush, and glare as she dares to look pleased.

"What the hell do you mean, she's not here?"

"She's on her way far away from you where she can be happy."

"Tell me you didn't betray me and help her leave."

"I did." My hands are around her throat before I can stop myself.

"Damiano, stop," my mother says, grabbing onto my arm.

Gabe is at my side. "Let my woman go."

I let go and say, "If anything happens to her, you're dead to me." I step back, hating myself, but not more than my sister at this moment. How could she have let the woman I love run away from me? I drop back to the chair with my head in my hands.

"We'll find her, Son," my father said.

"If you actually showed you cared, she wouldn't have wanted to leave," Grace says through her coughs.

"I'd shut your fucking mouth. I've had enough of this family's betrayal to last a lifetime. Blood means shit to me anymore, Ms. Valentino."

"Watch yourself, Son. You're both my children, and I love the two of you. This is not the same thing as my bastard father."

"No? Another betrayal. Another stab in the back by my own blood."

"You were going to get rid of her anyway. I was trying to save her heart. You're a man of your word, and you promised to let her go. Did you think she wanted to wait around until you finally tossed her out? You might not have a heart, but she does, and you don't get to break it over and over because you saved her from killing herself. I'd rather have her as a sister than you as a brother any day." She storms out of the room.

"She doesn't mean that."

"I don't give a fuck what she means. I want my wife."

"About damn time, but if you ever put your hands on my future wife, I'll forget who you are," Gabriele snarls.

"Good. You were looking like a weak-ass bitch."

"As angry as you were, you weren't hurting your sister, other than her feelings. Those I can work in my favor. Now back to your problem. I think I can help when it comes to finding your wife. I thought Gracie was being suspicious, and I had her followed when she went to Walmart, of all places."

"Walmart?"

"Yeah. I thought it was odd, but I thought she was being strange. She had ice cream. I asked her about it, and she was watching a TikTok thing and had to have it. Something they only had there."

"Let's check their surveillance."

She hasn't turned on the fucking phone Gracie had gotten her. What the hell? How am I supposed to track her whereabouts? Two fucking whole days have passed, and I'm not any closer to finding my wife.

"Son, what about her ring?" my father asks. My face

fell because it wasn't something I'd had time to achieve or thought of because I foolishly believed I'd let her go in the end, ring included.

"I didn't put a tracker in it."

"You used my jeweler, Fierro, correct?" My eyebrows shoot upward because I can already tell where his mind is going, and I hope that he's right. Although, since I'd been in a hurry, I doubt that's the case.

"Yes," I say. He calls him and puts it on speaker. "Fierro, my friend. I know you made a ring for my son quickly and as a special order, but I was wondering if you did what you always do for me?"

"A tracker?"

"Yes."

"All of my pieces are so expensive, Sir. It's a safety measure, but…" Fierro's nervous, but my heart jumps in my chest with the possibility.

"So, it's there?" I ask.

"Yes, but…" I cut him off before he started babbling.

"Is it possible to turn it on now, even with the ring not here? We're trying to find it."

"Yes, it's activated, but I hadn't wanted to pry."

"Thank you. Please send it to me ASAP. It's very important, and I will send you a bonus."

"It's not necessary, Sir. You are great to me and my family."

"I assure you, it's very appreciated and necessary." A few moments later, I have a trace running on my wife. It takes about twenty minutes, but a location comes up, and my sweet beauty is hiding away in Tallahassee.

"I'm sorry, Son. I wish I would have thought of that sooner."

"No. Not your fault. I have to find my wife." I'm out the door and on the road before anyone can stop me. It doesn't matter that we don't have Jones yet because getting Stella to safety is my only priority.

Leaning over her sleeping form, I watch my wife's tear-stained face. What the hell did she think she was doing? The risk she took to get away from me was foolish and dangerous. All for nothing, because there's no way I'd let her go now. She messed up. I thought she was an angel, but it seems she's a mischievous little thing, slinking away, planning to leave me with my unborn baby inside her. I hold the little stick in my hand, thinking of the baby devil growing inside of her, and suddenly the past, the betrayal, the pain, faded. All I want is my wife to say she'll stay by my side because I can't let her leave me.

She has no idea what the past three days and nights have been like. I almost choked the life out of my sister when I found out what she'd done. Never in my life have I been so pissed. Even my grandfather's accusations and attempt on my life meant nothing compared to her sending my wife away.

"Damiano," she whispers. My eyes widen and I think my little wife is awake, and that's when I realize she's still asleep. She whimpers a plea. "Why?" A sob comes from her, cracking something inside of me. The anger I had fades.

"Wake up, my little runaway. Angel, wake up."

"Dame," she gasps, swatting at me, but I'm too fast and I catch her hands, pinning her to the bed.

"Calm down, Wife, or you'll hurt yourself and our baby."

She freezes, parting her plump lips that I've missed so damn much. My mouth comes down on hers, kissing her with the passion of the past few days. She gives in without hesitation.

Suddenly, she halts and shoves me off her. "No. No. You can't do this to me. Please, just go. Please." Sobs wrack her chest, and I don't fucking like it.

"Don't cry. Shit." I stand and run my hands through my hair.

"I don't know how to stop." Every last bit of that wall between my heart and head has crumbled.

"Stella Valentino, will you stop and let me hold you for as long as I live?"

"Why, Damiano?" she sniffles out. I pull out my monogrammed handkerchief and wipe her tears.

"Because I love you. It took me a long time to realize it, but I do."

"Why should I believe you?"

"I should have known how I felt from the start. Yours is the first woman's touch I welcomed who wasn't blood." I was about to say family, but I had to bite that back.

"What? I don't understand."

"I may be the devil, but I have my own demons chasing me."

"The first woman to put her hands on me nearly sent me to my grave. I didn't tell her to touch me. Damn it, I even told her to get the fuck away from me, but the damage was done." Standing up again, I grab a bottle of water from her mini fridge and drink it before I sit down and tell the tale of young Damiano. By the time I'm finished, my sweet angel is crying.

"Sweet Stella, I didn't tell you that shit to have you crying again."

"I'm so sorry."

"You had to kill your grandfather."

"I thought for a long time that love made a man weak and foolish. My grandfather didn't even listen to his only grandson; he hadn't even given it a second thought. Then, my father gave his empire so easily to me to care for my mother and sister. All I saw was weakness. Until I met you...I wanted to have you and not at the same time. Use you for my pleasure, the longing, but I couldn't let you go. I didn't have anyone else, even if you thought so. You were too good to be like that bitch who nearly got me killed, but you were also the kind of woman who could make me give up everything at a word."

"I'd never."

"That's the thing. My father didn't do it because my mother asked; he did it because he couldn't get enough of her."

"Well, isn't twenty-something odd years long enough to pass on the reins or slow down to enjoy the finer things. Most people enjoy retiring."

"I didn't think so."

"And now?"

"Now, all I want to do is come home to you before the club even opens."

"Well, I could always pay you visits and keep you company. The lounge is quite comfortable, Mr. Valentino."

"Wife." A deep growl falls from my lips when a giggle falls from hers. I lean down and stare into her blue eyes and whisper, "I missed you so much."

She cups my jaw that could use a serious shave. "I missed you too. I like this, though."

"Do you?"

"Yes, it's sexy."

"Well, then, maybe I'll keep it a little longer, if you promise not to try some stupid shit like leaving me again."

"I never wanted to leave. I wanted to protect…"

"The baby from me?"

"I didn't know I was pregnant until now. My stomach being in knots could have been from my fear of leaving, but when I was here, I woke up sick, unable to stop. We weren't careful."

"Subconsciously, I wanted my child in you so I'd be forced to change my word. I'm the biggest fool."

"No, but why didn't fucking Gracie tell me about your past?" she snaps, trying to push me off again, but I'm not having that.

"She doesn't know," I sigh. As I say it, I feel like a bigger prick. Gracie has no idea how much of a betrayal her actions were. To her, Stella needed to be freed, and I needed to see the error of my ways.

"My relationship with my sister is in a bad place. I may have reacted poorly to her actions."

"Oh, no. Please tell me you didn't hurt her." I slam my eyes shut, unable to look at my wife. Her rejection is more than I can handle.

"Dame, tell me, is she alive?"

"Of course, but I might have been a little out of control. My father and Gabe stopped me from choking her."

"I need a moment."

"Please don't go."

"I'm not going anywhere." I give her the space she needs, but she doesn't move far. She only sits on the edge of the bed. "I feel so bad for going to her for help."

"Don't. This is between Grace and me. She knew what she was doing even if she didn't know about my grandfather. It was like she was doing it to spite me. To try and prove that she wasn't this sweet little naïve girl I thought she was."

"She did want to prove she isn't a child anymore."

"That's because she thought I didn't see her as more than a piece of meat for men and too weak to take care of herself, but I was only doing what big brothers do. A big brother with more power than any other."

"Sometimes it's hard to see what's in front of them." Stella releases a soft yawn.

"Oh, I'm sorry, little angel. It's been a trying day. Let's sleep."

"Will you stay?" she asks, sliding down under the covers.

"I'm not going anywhere without you."

A soft smile spreads over her face. "Can we go home tomorrow?" she asks, staring up at me as I undo my cuffs.

I consider returning, and despite the lack of traction on Jones's whereabouts, I'm not ready to head back. "No," I answer, undoing my shirt.

"No?" Sadness fills her eyes.

"Don't look so devastated, my angel. I owe you a proper honeymoon." I strip down to my boxers and slide under the covers, dragging my sweet wife into my arms. "Now close your eyes and get some sleep."

Holding her soothes some of the tension that has been there since the moment I knew she was gone. My phone rings as my queen falls asleep. "What is it?" I snarl at Benz. I've already learned from my people that Benz is a traitor. Anything he says should be taken with a grain of salt. His sister is that slut my father killed all those years ago. He may have changed his appearance completely, but a recent slip up gave it all away.

"There's movement outside the motel room. We're getting ready to move on it, and it's Rocco." I know damn well it isn't Rocco because we have eyes on him back in Miami, but my priority is getting Stella back.

"Shit. Hurry. I left Stella alone to get some dinner for her." I untangle myself from Stella, snatch my clothes off the floor, and dress. "Baby, wake up." I need you to put your clothes on fast. She starts to dress while I look for my bag, which is in the bathroom. My gun is in there. I'd been in such a rush that I'd forgotten I dropped it there when I saw the pregnancy test. My Sig is inside, ready to be clipped. I load the magazine as the door busts open. Fuck. I hide in the shower stall with the lights off.

"Ah, you little bitch." Fuck, Jones is inside. "I knew he would leave you unprotected. You were just a way to get back at Baker."

"What are you doing? I don't have anything you want."

"Oh, but you do. I've been waiting all these years for you. Young, ripe pussy that I've wanted to tap. After I take your pussy, I'll dump your dead body for your husband to find."

"Come near me, and you'll regret it."

"Hey, you'll let me get a turn too. I've waited so damn long for my revenge. Once we're done with her, his bitch little sister is next," Benz says.

"Find that prick before you get any pussy. He might not be armed, but he's going to come out swinging when he returns."

"Don't worry. I got my gun ready for that asshole." I'll drop both of them before they get their hands on her.

"Please, you don't have to do this."

"Yes, I do. God, you're a hotter version of your mother, and I'm sure that cunt is much tighter." I'm about to burst through the door when I hear the bed move.

"Come and get me, then, you pussy paying motherfucker." He snarls as I dip open the shower curtain. I'm about to shoot Jones in the back of the head when my wife stabs him in the eye with a fucking blade. One of my own blades. She shoves him off the bed, and I pounce out of the shower. He falls to the ground, howling, and the door opens.

"You stupid cunt. Bet you don't have any weapons left," Benz says.

"Wrong," she answers with a smile.

"You won't get anywhere near my sister," I growled, standing right behind him, and put a bullet right in his head. "That's for my little dark angels." His body slumps to the floor, and I stare at my gorgeous wife covered in blood looking so damn hot and not even remotely afraid.

With my phone to my ear, I make the call. "Gabe, I need a clean-up at the motel. Jones isn't a problem, and Benz has been disposed of. Have you dealt with our other problem?"

"Didn't have to do it."

"What do you mean?"

"She turned up at a hotel down the road. Body bloody ruined and drugged. It looks like she's been here for a day." I ended the call and set the phone down while keeping my eyes trained on my sexy wife. With a wag of my finger and my brows raised, I command, "You come here."

"We need to get this all cleaned up before the cops come," she insists, biting down on her bottom lip, looking nervous and yet so damn scandalous. There's something in her eyes that gives me pause, and I have questions.

"We will, but first I need to know you're okay."

"That felt so damn good." Her eyes light up. "And you look sexy, Damiano."

"Stella, baby. Are you horny?" I question, staring at my tiny wife with blood covering her, her staring up at me with nervous anticipation.

"Is that terrible?" Her round eyes ask for approval.

"No. Get that pretty little cunt over here and come in the bathroom so the devil can sully you up some more." I lift her off the bed and take her to the bathroom, closing the door and flipping the lock. Starting the shower, I slowly take off her clothes. "I need you right now, Stella." My hand fists around her throat and her pulse races.

"Dame, I need you."

I lift her into the small shower stall, slamming her tiny body against the cheap tile, breath leaving both of us as our mouths brush lightly across each other's. A feather kiss belies the hunger burning through my veins. "You'll always have me, my little hellfire. There's no way I'll ever let you go." Fuck, I tear off her panties and free myself from my boxers. Her entrance is sopping wet with need, desire clinging to my fingers, and I can't wait a moment longer before plundering my wife. It's been too many days. One full push, and I've claimed her again.

"Stella, you feel so perfect. Tell me what you need."

"Fuck me hard, Damiano. Use me." She pants as I pump harder into her tight slit, driving my aching cock deep into her heated depths. Sweat and water wash the blood off our bodies as we take our passion to a different level. Stella had been made for me, and I almost lost her.

"You would have found me." I didn't realize my slip up, but it doesn't matter because she's my better half, everything I'll never be and more.

"I love you," I grunt as I piston in and out of her slick cunt. "Come for me," I command, but it's more of a plea because I don't know how much longer I can hold out.

"Yes, my lord," she cries out, fingers spearing my soaked hair. My mouth clamps on her throat as I bellow out my orgasm, flooding her already seeded womb.

"Someone's in the room."

"I know." I slide out of my wife with a painful pop. Damn, maybe I was a little too rough with her.

"We'll be done soon, Boss." Adriano calls out. "Cops haven't been called. Do you need clothes in there?"

"Yes."

"When you're ready, knock and we'll turn around," my father says, and Stella turns beet red. "Clothes are on the table by the bathroom door."

"Thanks." I step out of the shower with a towel. Once I'm covered, I hand a towel to my wife but close the curtain. I don't want them to even get a single reflection of her. Rapping my knuckles on the cheap wood, I hear them stop working and a simple, "Ready?" come from my father.

I open the door and see a set of clothes for me. "We didn't want to touch her things, but there's her suitcase."

"I appreciate it." It's wise of them because they know how I feel about her. They shouldn't have been in here while I was drilling her, but the clean-up couldn't wait. If the cops or housekeeping showed up, there would be an issue. I own so many people in this state, but you never know who may want to start some shit.

"Get dressed, my love. I'll be out there dealing with the fallout." I kiss her hard and then step outside through a small opening. Jealousy and possessiveness will never end where she's concerned, even if I trust her implicitly.

The second my father sees me, he throws his arms around me. "It's so good to see you."

"I'm sorry," I say. It's not something I've said in many years, but it's days overdue.

"No, it's not me you owe an apology to, but I know it's not easy for you."

"You're right."

"How is she?"

"I underestimated my bride. She killed her stepfather."
Everyone stopped working and looked up at me.

"Holy shit. That was her handiwork?"

"Yes, my little angel has a dark side."

"Remind me not to piss her off," Adriano says, tossing his hands up.

"So I'm going to be a grandfather?"

"I hope a really great one."

"Me too. Your mother's going to be excited. I have to call her before she freaks out, though. She's been messaging me, waiting for an update since I followed you."

"Why did you?"

"You're my son, and you needed me, even if you don't think so. I know what it's like to be in love, and I'd do anything to keep your mother safe. Even if your sister did what she did with the best intentions, the second Stella Valentino left the house unprotected, she became a huge target."

"Thank you." The bathroom door opens, and my angelic bride walks out, looking perfectly sweet even though everyone in the room knows something darker lies underneath, and I couldn't be prouder and now my dick is back at it. We need to be alone again.

CHAPTER TWENTY-FIVE

DAMIANO

We spent a week in Barbados, enjoying the beach, the water, and most importantly, each other. I made love to Stella every moment I could, but it is finally time to return home. She isn't feeling so well, and after a quick check-up with an island physician, morning sickness is getting to my gorgeous wife.

Besides, I still have one more person to deal with. A traitor above all. Rocco. He has played us more than the others. He's been waiting so patiently for my return that I have to welcome him with special treatment. After I take care of that treacherous bastard, I have a massive apology to make.

"Sleepy, beautiful?" I whisper, watching Stella stretch out on the plane lounger.

"Yes, so sleepy." She lets out an adorable yawn like a cat.

"Rest. We'll be home in two hours."

We took our private jet because I refused to share her with anyone else or risk someone attacking. Our security has been tight after the other set of fires. Benz has been involved with the help of Baker, but I doubt they are the only ones. My enemies list is long, including Salazar's family. Word has gotten out that he's missing, and I'm the last person he'd gone to see.

"Sounds wonderful." She sighs, snuggling up in just one of my shirts. We didn't even make it to the landing strip before I was balls deep in her, tearing off her sundress. I don't know what it is, but seeing her in dresses sends my cock up to full mast. I summon the flight attendant and request a blanket for my wife. She's about to put it on her, but that's my pleasure.

I work for the rest of the flight, twirling a glass of whiskey while I consider the probability that my sister might not want to speak to me. Will that harm her friendship with Stella? They were so close.

The flight attendant comes in to remind us to buckle in for landing. "Thank you. I'll wake my wife."

"Yes, Mr. Valentino."

"Time to rise, Angel. We're about to land," I whisper, kissing her lips until she moans and opens up for me.

"I'm awake," she sighs, opening her pretty blues, and wraps her arms around my neck. How the fuck did I ever think I could let her go? She sits up and is about to buckle herself in, but I drag her over to the seat next to me. While she was sleeping, I allowed her to lay so far away, but now that she's up, I want her by my side.

"What are you doing?" she asks, pressing her hands on my shoulders so she doesn't fall.

"There's no reason for you to be so far away from me." A smile spreads across her gorgeous face.

"Yes, boss man." She nips at the scruff on my chin. "I'm going to miss this."

"I'll keep it trimmed close just for you." I rub my cheek against her cheek.

"It better be just for me, Mr. Valentino," she snarls, jabs my chest.

"Always all for you."

"So, Body Count has a totally different meaning," she teases. After everything she has seen and learned over the past six weeks, it's no secret that I enjoy the kill.

"Yes," I confess.

"My devil."

"My angel."

The plane taxis, and then we finally exit. As we head to the vehicle, Gabe comes out to take our things. Then, my sister jumps out of the front passenger seat. I'm about to speak to her, but she throws her arms around me. "I'm sorry, Hummingbird."

"I'm sorry, Damiano. So sorry. She could have died. I didn't realize what I did. Dad told me about Grandpa. I hope he rots in hell."

"It's okay. I promise. You see, my beautiful wife was never going to get away from me. Ever."

"I knew it the second you stormed the house. I'm just sorry I didn't know it sooner."

"Me too."

"Well, now that we got that out of the way, I need hugs

from my auntie maker." She throws her arms around Stella. "Mom told me," she squeals.

"Of course she did. What are the rules in our family? Everything is a secret as a Valentino, but come on, this one isn't that big of one." She huffs.

"I know. My baby will be coming soon. Now, let's get somewhere out of the open. We might not have the immediate threat of the Joneses anymore, but that doesn't mean there aren't others looming."

"Speaking of, Chief Inspector Rodriguez wanted to see you regarding the warehouse and the docks."

"Of course he does. The piece of shit doesn't give a damn about the truth. He's on the take for someone, and I want to know who. I'm tired of his games." I help my wife into the back seat, while Gracie sits up front with Gabe who takes her hand in his as we drive off. It's then I spot the fucking stone on her finger.

"Is there something the two of you forgot to mention?" Stella blurts out.

"Oh, Dame didn't tell you?" Gabriele remarks, smirking from behind his shades.

"No."

"I asked Gracie to be my wife."

"Wow, that's wonderful," Stella squeals, but then gives me a glare.

"What? I kind of forgot since we were busy celebrating all week." I lift her onto my lap, rubbing my ever-present erection on her tight ass.

"We have a lot to celebrate," Gracie says.

"We so do." My mouth latches onto my wife's throat, marking her soft, sun-kissed skin.

"Mom, is looking forward to throwing a fabulous wedding and a baby shower, so don't give her no shit, Damiano."

"I'm not." I toss my hands up, grumbling to myself. "When the fuck did I get weak around these women?"

My wife leans in and whispers, "You're not weak, darling. You're my dark hero and definitely so damn hard." A moan escapes her parted lips, and my hand covers her mouth.

"Only for me, Wife. Only for me."

"Always."

We settle into the house, but there's somewhere important I need to be. "Love, I'm sorry to do this now that we're back home, but I have to go to work."

"Is this about Rocco?"

"Yes."

"Then you know I'm all for it. It's been a long time coming, so do what you must. Besides, when are you opening up the club again?"

"The glass has been replaced and I'll be inspecting it tomorrow, so hopefully we open by the weekend. That doesn't mean your sexy ass can come in with those half-clothed outfits again."

"What if I want to be spanked and thoroughly fucked five ways from Sunday?"

"That I can do, but plucking other men's eyeballs out takes a lot of time out of my busy schedule, so it would be good if you'd just behave."

"Fine. I'll be a good girl and waiting in bed." She pouts prettily, tilting her head up with her eyes gleaming, full of mischief. I can't wait to dispose of my former associate so I can satisfy my willing bride.

We arrive at the location, and the sight of Rocco brings joy to my eyes. So far, everyone's death has been unsatisfying to me, and almost all not at my own hand. He has betrayed more than myself; he sent one of my oldest allies to his death, leaving his family without a father and husband. That was more than distasteful—it deserved retribution, and I will be delivering it tonight.

"It's so good to finally catch up with you," I say. His eyes widen and he moves to run, only to slam into Adriano's brick-wall frame. See, unlike the others, Rocco has never been tied up or trapped, just monitored. We didn't want him to stew. I wanted a surprise when I finally met him. I didn't want the off chance of him pulling a Baker. Adriano is the best and made sure that he never lost sight of him.

"Where are you going? We've been looking for you for so long, it's a wonder we managed to find you alive after all of Jones's and Baker's acquaintances have seemingly died or disappeared." He's shaking, and all the color in his olive face has faded, turning him a hideous pale gray.

"I only just broke free from them. I tried to get back, but they had me tied up."

"The fact that you lack respect for me says one thing, but your own lack of respect for yourself says a lot more. You're a big pussy and full of utter denial that you're about to die for your sins against me and mine."

Adriano effortlessly holds him still as Rocco attempts to struggle away from his grasp. My first gut shot feels incredible. Blow after blow, I deliver shots to his body, working my fist into his frame, letting the sound of his bones crack play like music to my ears. "That's for my wife; that's for the time you've kept me on the hunt; that's for ruining my businesses." Each blow wears him down, but I don't give in because his death will mean I get to sleep easier, even if it's temporary.

"Come on. If you stop it, I'll tell you who is after you," he groans through the pain.

"Go on and spill, Rocco. It won't save your life, but it will spare your pain. If the information is good." As he tries to breathe, he spills his guts. Once I've gotten what I need, I end his life with a quick bullet to the head. "Payment for services rendered."

"Now—home, or are you ready to pay a visit to him?"

"No, I need eyes on him. Rocco can't be believed, but I have no intention of keeping him alive a moment longer. Something isn't adding up, so dig a little more. However, I need to make a pit stop before I go home and see my wife." It's time to right some other wrongs.

CHAPTER TWENTY-SIX

STELLA

It was already morning when Damiano returned from his mission to dispose of a traitor, and I missed him terribly. It's the first night we haven't slept together since we confessed our feelings. What if we go back to where we were?

"Good morning, beautiful." He leans in and kisses me as I drink my coffee. "I missed you." He takes my coffee and sets it down.

"I missed you too," I breathe against his chest.

"Here—I bought you something on the way here." I take the gift bag and open it, nearly sending it to the floor in surprise when I see what's inside, but he catches it. "Whoa, let's set it down."

I pull out the cell phone and tablet. "You got me these?"

"Don't sound so excited. I already feel like a bastard

about leaving you stranded without basic technology for this long."

"These aren't basic. That thing I had was basic." He frowns, and I know the running away bothers him, so I brush his still scruffy face. "I love you, Dame."

His eyes darken, and his breathing grows heavy. "Say it again, and I'll show you how to use it."

My own pulse quickens throughout my body, heart beating out of control, but I stay poised because I'm loving this new side of my husband. "I'll say it again and you can kiss me."

"I was going to do that anyway." He sets the devices on the counter and pulls me in for a deep kiss. His fingers spear through my hair, holding me firmly while dominating my mouth. It isn't until I'm gasping that he's pulling away only to get some breathing room.

"So…" His eyebrows raise, licking his lips like he's had a delectable snack.

"Oh, so how does it work?" I tease. He gives me a stern face that would rattle most men, but I've never been truly afraid of this man. "Fine." Rolling my eyes, I say, "I guess I can repeat myself. I love you."

"Good, because I have a feeling you are going to make me repeat myself all the damn time."

"Yes, because I know how much you don't like it." He sits down on the seat next to me, then scoops me up and sits me in his lap. "I know how much you like this."

"Maybe a little too much. We're going to repeat a lot of lessons today."

"A lot." I moan as he attacks my neck with kisses.

It tales all afternoon for me to get the hang of his

phone and tablet explanations, but it doesn't matter because the three orgasms in between were so worth the spankings for not paying attention.

"Dinner will have to be continued, *Dolcezza.*"

"Work stuff?"

"Yes. There's an urgent matter, or I wouldn't be leaving you."

"You know I understand completely."

"The club opens tomorrow, so I'd like you to come with me."

"Really?"

"Yes, but nothing like you were wearing the last time."

"Okay. I promise I'll be a good girl. Or maybe not."

"I fucking heard that shit. Just so you know, there's no one going to let you slide on that shit because I will be escorting you to the club myself."

"Damn it." He scowls at me, which only makes me grin.

"I'll call your troublemaker sister and ask what acceptable attire for the club is."

He shakes his head like he's had enough of me, but he still comes back for more, returning to my chair and cupping my chin. "If that's the case, maybe you would be better asking my mother. She knows how to keep my father from killing anyone. I've buried a lot of bodies since I met you, and I'll gladly bury thousands more, Cara." He's right, because she's gorgeous and doesn't even look like she has grown-ass kids with a figure that matches mine or her daughter's. You wouldn't know that she was in her fifties.

CHAPTER TWENTY-SEVEN

DAMIANO

I'm still not happy about her outfit, but then again, what would make me pleased is a fucking sack on her while we're in my club. Although, my bride deserves to wear only the best, so tonight's gown is gorgeous as hell on her soft skin. "You look fabulous, Stella."

"Yes, you look stellar," Hummingbird says, bouncing around our bedroom like the little bird she is.

"Don't you have a home?" I sneer at my sister.

She just sticks out her tongue and goes to her makeup bag, waving it at me. "I do, but I promised I wouldn't leave until I did her makeup, so stop being a pest and go entertain my fiancé."

"Keep it up, and I'll keep him busy on assignments until your wedding."

"You're not a very nice big brother."

"Well, I know what he does to you in private and I should kill him for it, so I think I'm pretty nice."

"Whatever. You need to leave us so I can make your wife beautiful."

"She's already beautiful."

"I just wanted to hear you say it." She winks at Stella, and I let out a laugh. I've been beat, so I look for my men. The risk for the club will be low tonight because police will be all around. Still, I can't let my guard down when it comes to my wife.

Twenty-five long minutes later, my wife and sister finally traipse down the steps, and I'm floored by the beauty before me. It's not what she did to her; it's the glow on her face. She's happy.

Meeting my wife there, I close the distance and take her hand in mine before bringing it to my lips. "So perfect. Are you ready, Mrs. Valentino?"

"Yes," she says, biting the edge of her bottom lip.

As soon as we get to the waiting armored town car, I say, "Tell me what's going on. That light's missing."

"Actually, I'm a little nervous."

Is she afraid of the danger? I'd die for her, and I'll tear apart anyone who comes between us. Cupping her chin, I look into her eyes to read her well. "Why?"

She blushes, and I want to fuck her on the leather seats beneath us. "I've actually never been dancing. Will you dance with me?"

"How about we dance alone in our private VIP booth?"

"I'd like that." She leans her pretty head on my shoulder as we drive into the city.

The drive to the club is fraught with tension as my

phone blows up with messages and calls. I learn a lot about my former soldiers. The details come in from Nico, and they're not good. Benzino was not only related to that cunt that came between my family and nearly cost me my life, but Rocco was too. They were relatives of another family —one I suddenly had an unknown beef with.

We'll see how long that lasts; a war will be had. I've never lost before, and this time, a lot more is at stake. A future.

"Now what's wrong with you?"

"Nothing."

"Don't lie to me, Damiano Marciano Valentino."

"It's nothing for you to worry about, is what I mean. Tonight, I want you to enjoy being the only woman ever on my arm to sit in my lap and dance in my arms."

"Fine, but I'm not a wilting flower."

"That doesn't mean you need to be involved in the big-boy problems. I need you and my baby well protected."

"Of course, if that's what you want. I'll do it, just don't tell me nothing's wrong when I can see it. I'm naïve to a lot, but reading a man's face is something I've grown very used to." She doesn't have to explain that response to let me know she lived with warding off the next round of abuse. Watching her tongue and expressions kept her from trouble, so she knew to be on guard.

Bringing her hand to my lips, I kiss the back of it and apologize. "I'm sorry, Amore. I'll try to remember."

We arrive at the club ten minutes later, and my wife is a little less frazzled. Cameras and police are all around because tonight's the grand reopening and everyone wants details. "Mr. Valentino, Mr. Valentino, can we get a word?"

a reporter shouts. She doesn't wait, of course. "Is it true that someone has finally landed Miami's notorious elusive bachelor?"

"If that's your impolite way of asking if this lovely woman is my wife, then yes. My wife, Stella. Now, if you'll excuse us, we have a club to open. You may come in, but of course, cameras and recording equipment are to be left outside."

"What about the fires? Any answers? Will there be trouble?"

"I certainly hope not, but as you can see, security and police have been amplified. I'm not a fire investigator, so I don't have answers on the fires. Now, excuse us." I lead Stella away from the woman who has taken an enviable stare at my wife.

"Jealousy is ugly on such a beautiful woman," Stella says to the reporter.

I lean and whisper, "Mio angelo oscuro." Stella smiles wickedly. Possessiveness looks great on her.

I lead her in, and we walk around to the bar. "Everyone, gather around." Feet shuffle quickly as they tend to when I'm here. "I'd like to make a formal introduction before we open the doors. This beautiful woman you have seen here before. However, I haven't properly introduced her as my wife, Stella Valentino. She should be treated as you would me, and you know what that means. If anyone dares approach her, I want to know. Understood?"

They quickly cheer and agree. After they greet her with the respect fitting my wife, I lead her around to inspect the club. It's something I do almost every time I come in. The place is perfect, including the extra cameras I added just in case we get some unwelcome visitors. My office has been triple-swept and thoroughly cleaned after the supposed fire at the club.

"It's time to open. Do you want to go to the door, or would you rather wait in our lounge?"

"I have to use the ladies' room."

"Okay, but use the one in my office." I kiss her lips and then nod toward Adriano. "Escort my wife upstairs, please."

"Of course." She follows his lead to the steps, and I watch as he acts the perfect guard for her. I'm glad there are some I can truly trust with her. Especially that big motherfucker. The next ten minutes are hectic as we let in the VIPs, and then finally I head up to my office. Adriano's standing guard outside. "I told her it was best just to wait for you inside."

"Good." I turn the knob and see the sexiest sight. My pretty wife is sitting on the edge of my desk holding one of my blades, twirling it in her hand. "Are you planning to off me tonight?"

"No. Adriano wanted to make sure I was protected, so he showed me where you keep the special hiding spot."

"Smart. You're really good with knives, but maybe we'll take you to the range. How would you like that?" I take the knife from her and set it down.

"Anything to keep this one safe." She rubs her belly.

"Hopefully we don't have that problem, Mrs. Valentino, but for now, I owe you a dance."

"Do you have any music in here?" We have speakers in the club that connect to my office, but I can change it so I don't have to hear the shit out there. I put on something slow and pull my wife into my arms. Holding her is always a pleasure, but watching others in the club dancing had never filled me with envy until I crossed paths with my little angel.

The song comes to an end, and she stares up into my eyes with a happiness that I can latch onto for my own. The only light I let in. "This is wonderful, Dame. Can we stay like this for another song?"

"For a while longer," I whisper over her head, wanting to spend the rest of the night just the two of us. "You and I will have our own little night this week."

"It's a date, Mr. Valentino," she says, brushing her lips on my shaved chin. I had to clean up for the club, but I didn't leave it completely bare. "I want that between my thighs."

"At your service." I stop dancing and go to lift her on the desk, but she stops me.

"Not now, silly."

"Can't blame a guy. Look what you do to me." I rub my painful erection on her mound.

"We better go outside and see what's going on before we get carried away."

"Sounds wonderful." We exit the office and join Gabe and Gracie in the VIP booth with Adriano, who is surveying the floor below.

"Anything going on?"

"Nothing. The club is running as smoothly as ever, like nothing has ever changed, but we know differently." We all understand that's the farthest from the truth because not only has Rocco betrayed us, but the fire was a ruse while

Benz had snuck inside and tried to break into the safes to steal information they believed was here, as if I didn't have safety precautions everywhere. Sending in the fire department was their attempt to get more access to closed-off areas, but they underestimated my actual firewalls and my digital ones.

"We need drinks," I say. "Amore, you want water? A virgin cocktail?"

"Water." I press the button for service, and seconds later Sasha is up the steps. "Yes, Boss. What can I get you all tonight?"

"A refill for Gracie and Gabe, water, my usual, and…" I point to Adriano. "A chocolate milk."

"I'm not trying to go to bed. I'll take a water," he grumbles. "I'll be back in a minute." She's not gone long before returning with Adriano taking the tray. "Here you go. Will you be needing a refill in fifteen?"

"Sounds good. Thanks."

"Yes, Boss. Have a good evening." She nods and takes the now empty tray.

"How long has she been working here?"

"Since we opened the club. She's the best server and knows not to try shit, so she's the only one who gets to come up here to take orders."

"She seems nice. She told off Camille when we came here that night."

"The other guy didn't care and served us in a heartbeat." I wanted to smash his head in, but it was his job, so what the fuck was I supposed to do?

"Let's dance," Gracie says. She grabs Stella's hand and drags her away from me. A growl comes from deep within.

"My wife doesn't dance in the club. You can have your own dance parties, but fuck if I want these pussies staring at her."

"Same, babe."

"Fine—then you both better dance with us." She grabs Gabe, Stella takes my hand, and we dance in the VIP lounge. It's surprisingly incredible having my wife shake her ass all over me while we find a nice rhythm to the music. Quickly I face the other direction because there's no way I want to see my sister grind up on my best friend and underboss the way my wife is on me.

Two hours later a yawn escapes my wife, and I wonder if this was a bad idea. She's pregnant, and it's late. We pop down in the seats and drink a little more.

"Do you want to head home?" I ask.

"No, it's your special night."

"Baby, you're sleeping on me," I tell her, trying to explain that she's got nothing left in her.

"I don't mean to kill your buzz," she huffs. She stands up and nearly trips over the table in front of us.

"We're leaving," I snarl. I won't have her risking her health just to please me.

"No, you stay. I'm going home."

"No, I'll take you home."

"No. You have to work, and I'm tired. I can call an Uber or something."

"The hell you can. You all have a great night. My angel and I need to tuck in our baby for the night." I shoot my driver a message to be ready in two minutes, and then I scoop her in my arms and carry my sleepy wife out of the club through the back while security watches our exit.

We're about twenty minutes on the road when an unsettling feeling hits me. There are two vehicles following us, and they haven't broken off.

I'm on the phone to Gabe and Adriano at the same time. "We're being followed."

"Fuck. Any ideas on who?"

"No. Any movement on Rodriguez?"

"No, he goes to work and does his job. His reports on the fires don't add up, but everything else shows up clean."

"What's going on, Damiano?" Stella whimpers when the sounds of guns go off.

"Fuck, we're on our way."

"The vehicle's armored, Amore. We're going to be okay." I yell to my driver, "Filo, drive faster and get us to my estate."

I call my father. "We're being chased about ten from my house."

"Adriano sent out the code. Men will be on their way as well as at the estate. Mi figlio, be safe."

"I am trying to protect my family." Rage boils in me. As soon as I get these pricks, hell will be paid.

When they realize their weapons won't penetrate, they go for ramming and that's enough to set me off, but my driver is an expert. He maneuvers through their attempted pits. We're nearly to the estate, and then our gates slide open for us to get in. As we do, I say, "Stay down, Angel. It's time for the devil to play."

I pull out the hidden launcher, and the vehicle only comes to a stop long enough to get in my sights. Bastards. I shoot it, sending it up and landing on the SUV, turning it to molten metal in seconds.

The other vehicle quickly speeds off, but I have surveillance that will be of good use. We don't approach until the all-clear is given, but I wait before I take my wife inside our estate. Filo holds off until I tell him to let her out because there's no way I want anyone to be lying in wait. My father and his men pull up in a dozen vehicles and join my men around the property, guns ready.

My body is vibrating with rage, seething as I consider the ramifications. We were obviously observed leaving the club, and it could have been at a distance because it's a very popular area, but it doesn't change a damn thing. War is what they want, and war is what they'll get.

Walking to the vehicle, I open the door and my wife is no longer inside, but neither is my driver. "Son of a bitch. They're gone. Where did they go? Get me cameras. He's taken my wife."

"No, he hasn't," Stella sighs, coming from the line of trees. Her lip is busted, and her forehead is bleeding.

"Amore, Angel." I drag her to me and see the knife from my office.

"He's involved. He dragged me away, and I'm glad I grabbed the knife."

"Gun lessons tomorrow," I growl, holding her to my chest, breathing harshly as I think about all the fucking heads that are about to roll.

"Get her inside and protected," my father says.

"She needs a medic," I grunt. "Where's that piece of shit?"

"He's not going to be able to speak," Stella says with a weak smile.

"Good girl." I look down at her, tipping her chin, and then her face contorts.

"My belly hurts, Dame." She collapses in my arms. I rush her into the house, but she really needs a hospital. My housekeeper meets me at the door and leads the way to our room.

"Let me get her cleaned up." She's carrying the first-aid kit already, and another maid brings over wet washcloths. Normally I never let all these people in my room, but nothing matters but my wife's care. "Please back up, Mr. Valentino." I move around and give her some space.

"Stella, can you tell me where you're hurt besides your head?"

"My stomach."

"Okay. Can I check your panties?" She nods, and my housekeeper starts to lift Stella's dress.

"Close the door," I snarl. The maid shuts the door as she checks Stella's underwear.

"Good news so far—I don't see any blood. I can't say anything, but blood might mean a miscarriage." That's really fucking good to know, but she said it's just a sign.

"Still, she needs a doctor." The maid wipes Stella's forehead, and then they clean the cut. There's a nasty bruise on her face that sets my teeth on edge.

A rapid knock at the door sends me to my feet. I rush to the door and nearly tear it off the hinges. "Oh my God," my sister sobs, rushing into the room followed by my mother and then the doctor.

"She needs medical attention now. She's pregnant," I order.

"I need everyone, including you, to give me space." Everyone steps back and the doctor takes over. "Mrs. Valentino, I'm going to touch you."

As much as I should be pissed that he's a man examining my wife, nothing matters because I want her better. He palpitates around her belly and looks.

"Can you explain what happened?" He checks the wounds on her head and the scratches on her arms, most taken care of by my staff. "He pointed a gun at me the second Dame exited the vehicle, and then told me to exit quietly or he'd shoot me before Damiano could reach me." She sobs, but then catches her breath and continues. "I slid out with my purse on, and he yanked me through the tree line. I knew I didn't have much time, so I fell to the ground and then he hit me with the gun, telling me to get up or he'd kill me right on the spot."

I take her hand, hoping that will give us both the strength—her to continue telling the rest, and me from not going insane right now and killing every damn man I see.

"It was fuzzy for a moment, but then I had enough. Sliding the switchblade you gave me tonight from my purse, I popped it open and stabbed him in the throat, pulled it out, and then shoved it in his hand that he had the gun in. He fell on me, and that's when I pushed off and ran back."

"Fucking badass, girl. My sister-in-law is ice cold. Who would have ever imagined?"

"My dark angel."

"How far along are you, my dear?"

"Less than six weeks or so."

"Are you cramping?"

"No."

"Okay. Well, I'd like to run some bloodwork and stuff, but overall, the injuries are superficial. Fatigue and stress might be why you fainted, and the pain might be minor. We can't know just yet, but we can test your levels. Rest, and I will check on you soon."

"What about my baby?"

"You're not very far along, with no blood present, and lack of cramping is a good sign. My palpitations don't show much at this stage. Labs will be better to give us a detailed timeline. I suggest you see your OBGYN as soon as possible. As much as I'd like to help, I'm not a specialist in that area."

"I understand." He is the guy we call for gunshots and shit, but he was the closest, and frankly I'm afraid to let her leave the estate.

"Can we get the doc here with an ultrasound machine?" Hummingbird asks.

"I don't see why not," I answer.

"I have a coworker who I trust. She's a great doctor, and discreet."

"Fantastic. Send her over first thing in the morning with the equipment."

I escort him to the door. "Is she truly okay?"

"Physically, yes. Emotionally, I don't know her, so that would be your call."

"Then she'll be just fine. Thank you."

"Congratulations, Damiano. You've landed a perfect wife."

"That I did." Now it's time to make people pay.

I turn to everyone in the room. "Now, I appreciate

everything you all have done, and it will not go unnoticed. However, I would like to be alone with my wife." They all nod in understanding before they leave. Gracie squeezes my shoulder and kisses my cheek. I nod and then lock the door behind them.

"Damiano." The light whimper that comes from my wife hardens my heart. I kick off my shoes and slide off my coat. Climbing into bed, I hold her lightly. "I want you to stay with me, but I can see the venom in those devilishly beautiful eyes."

"I'm fighting my urges."

"Don't fight them, Damiano. I love you, so all that I ask is that you come back to me safely for me and our little one."

"I can't lose you."

"I'll be safe in our bed with someone watching the door. Maybe I could stay with your parents."

"No, you're not leaving our room. I'll send them here. You will be watched. Let me get you out of this and changed." I slip her out of her dress and then pull out the dress shirt I left on the chair from this afternoon and slide it over her body, buttoning it up.

"I love wearing your clothes."

"You look sexy in it too." I kiss her softly and then it grows, but then she yips and I remember her busted mouth. "Damn it. I'm sorry, Angel."

"Don't worry about me. Go on and take care of your family. Show them the devil, and I'll be waiting like a good girl."

"You better be."

It's a struggle to pull away, but I need answers and

there's one motherfucker who is going to give them to me, or he and his family are dead. Whipping open my bedroom door, I find my entire family waiting there on pins and needles. "Stay here with her. Don't fucking leave her side until I return. Something happens, I want to know. A cough, sneeze, anything."

My mother pulls me in for a hug. "Calm yourself, and remember you are no good to her dead. Keep a steady head and get these bastards. Your father has been doing this longer. He'll show you how vendettas work." She gives me a sinister smirk, and I wonder how much I don't know about my youth and the time I was unconscious.

CHAPTER TWENTY-EIGHT

DAMIANO

He's in his office at this late hour, which doesn't quite surprise me because what we do in the dark comes to light. I creep in while my men make sure there isn't a soul who saw my presence.

"Good evening, Rodriguez."

"Valentino. What are you doing in here? You shouldn't be here." His eyes are as wide as saucers, almost coked out. He peers outside, searching for something.

"Why would that be?" I challenge the high-and-mighty prick to tell the truth. This time, there will be no easy death until I get the answers I came for. Stella's everything to me, and I'll destroy the world to bring her peace.

"You shouldn't be here," he doubles down.

"Is that because I should be dead?"

"What? No." I rush on him in a heartbeat, lifting him off his feet and into the air before slamming him violently against the wall, sending his framed awards falling as the worthless shits should.

"I swear I have no idea what you're talking about, but if they see you here, they'll kill my wife and kids," he chokes out.

"Well, they tried to kill mine tonight, so excuse me if I don't give a fuck."

"Please, I didn't have anything to do with your wife and I didn't know you had children."

"She's pregnant."

"I just haven't ruled on the fires yet."

"Why?"

"They want you to turn over territory and property to them. They figured you'd be weakened with my office breathing down your neck when we accuse you of crimes. They have leverage. I wouldn't play ball, but they took my family tonight." The tears in his eyes are real and vulnerable. His family portrait on his desk reminds me that a man will do whatever to protect his own. Even someone who is dedicated to the right side of the law.

"Who are they, and where did they take them?"

"The Otero Family." Fucking Salazar's relatives. That piece of dirt's relations are behind all of this. I think back to that encounter in my office. No, it wasn't because I offed that prick because they never came after him; hell, no one even bothered to look for him. He was just another pawn of theirs. They were just stealing from me, and he was their first test.

"Which Otero took your family?"

"Miguel."

"If you're playing me…"

"I'm not. I swear. I had proof it was arson and even who started two of the fires, but I got threatened before I could report it. One of their family members works for fire department."

"By tomorrow, there will be no more Oteros," I promise. "We're going to leave. You don't speak to no one."

We walk out and wait because if they're watching him, someone will be in contact shortly. Adriano pretends to drive away when a man walks back into the station and into the office. We follow and listen. "What the fuck did you say to them?"

"Nothing. He threatened me, wanting to know who started the fires. I told him it's not that easy. It's not like people write their names on the fires."

"He let you live?" that bastard Otero says, voice laced with suspicion. He doesn't know I'm about to get his ass.

"Killing a city official investigating his properties doesn't seem like a smart move for him."

"What else did you tell him? He had to want more."

"Nothing. I swear."

"You're fucking lying, Cousin."

"We're not family anymore. Family doesn't do this to each other." Family?

I nod to Adriano, so he goes inside and pounces on Otero, knocking him out cold. I enter behind him and stare at Rodriguez. "Hiding secrets."

"I don't consider them family and haven't for two decades, and this is what they consider family—taking mine." We spent the next three hours taking down one house after another until we found the one that had Rodriguez's family.

"Miguel... Come out, come out, wherever you are," I greet the bastard, wanting a confrontation, craving it.

"You think you're slick, Valentino, but your men easily turn on you." He comes out of the shadows with Rodriguez's wife in his arms, her neck bleeding, but she's alive. "You aren't the top dog anymore. I am."

"Bullshit. So I had a couple of pussies out of thousands. One who wanted revenge, and two looking for handouts. They got what they deserved."

"What? Filo's dead?"

"Yes. He shouldn't have put his hands on my wife."

"I'm going to enjoy fucking that bitch once you're dead. She looked so damn good, and if that stupid Benz had done his job, she would have been in my grasp sooner, screaming my name on her knees." I've had enough. He thinks he's hitting a nerve, and truthfully and he is, but I'm deadly and so much more.

"She'd never. She'd slice your balls off first, and you'd be crying her name, begging to be saved."

"We'll see." He shoves Rodriguez's wife and lifts a gun, but he's too fucking slow. I shoot him between the eyes. He falls back but manages to get a shot off, hitting me in the arm. I've been hit before, so I brush it off because I need to get Rodriguez's family to him before some of Otero's allies come looking for revenge.

The little kids are petrified, but we work quickly to get them out of here and to safety before wreaking havoc on the rest of the family.

It isn't until the next morning that I'm able to return

home and see my wife after destroying over half the Otero Family. There is more to do than kill all the heads and anyone who opposes my takeover, but I have an angel to look after.

The doc bandages me up, and then I head up to the only place I want to be. Opening my bedroom door with my father and Gabe following behind, we find all three of our ladies curled up on the bed together, clearly having kept each other company all night.

"Come on, sleeping beauties. It's time to wake up and go home," my father says.

Yawns rip through the room and it's actually adorable, but I want them the fuck out of my room so I can hold my sweet kitten. My father scoops up my mother, and Gabe does the same with Gracie. They all leave, and I strip down to my boxers to cuddle my wife.

"I love you, Angel."

"I love you, my dark prince."

EPILOGUE

STELLA

"**S**tella, what do you think of this color?" My mother-in-law shows me a swatch with three colors, pointing to the middle. I love it, but I'm still not sure. Damiano has given me way too much control in the house, something I've never had before, and it's overwhelming. Tears fill my eyes, and I leave the room.

I rush to our bedroom and close the door, hating my reaction because I've just embarrassed myself. The quick movement of my husband's expensive shoes across the hall and into our bedroom startles me. He sits on the bed and reaches over to tip my chin. "Angel, look at me."

"Damiano, I can't." With my stepfather, I never had any choices in a single thing. After three months with my husband, there isn't a thing he doesn't allow me to do when it comes to the house. The chef comes to me about meals, any possible changes, and so does the housekeeping staff. It's crazy how much power I've been given. Even my new cell phone has every bit of capability as anyone else's. Not that I know what to do with most of it. Reading and texting Gracie and Damiano are my biggest uses of the device.

"Is my face hideous now? I mean, I can't do this. I'm not good at this much responsibility." I'm so overwhelmed.

"Wife, enough." I'm on his lap with a gasp. "Don't doubt yourself. You're fantastic at everything you've tried so far. You're only picking colors for the baby's room."

"But this is the third time I've changed my mind, and I'm probably driving your mother insane."

He chuckles, "Sweet angel, the only thing she cares about is that you're healthy, and that little one coming out so she can spoil him."

"But the painters…"

He presses his hand to my lips. "Can do whatever the fuck I tell them to do. They work for us, and if they've said something to you, you better tell me and I'll take care of it."

"They didn't, but…"

"No more buts. Although this one is very nice," he growls, rubbing my ass on his growing length. "Enough. I have some matters to deal with, so you can just relax, or you can go back and play with all the pretty palates and eat. I don't want you going without lunch."

"I love you, Damiano."

"I hope so. I live for those words now." He stares into my eyes, and then it's his eye color that has grown to be my favorite. We share a deep, passionate kiss. When we break apart, I say, "Walk me back down. I'm ready to go back and redecorate."

"That's my good girl." I love being his good girl and his bad girl, which he enjoys as well.

By the end of the week, the room has been completed and it's time to show him what I picked. "So let's see what you selected." He opens the door, and his mouth drops open. "Wow, it's perfect. That's a beautiful gray."

"I hope he loves it because it's the color of his daddy's eyes."

He turns to me and smiles. "My eyes?" A glint sparkles in those devilish grays that have enchanted me since we met.

"Yes. They've always captivated me, Damiano. I find comfort, love, and desire in them," I confess.

"Darling, beautiful wife, you couldn't have made this room any more special except when we settle our little son's head down to rest for the first time. I love you so much." He sweeps me into his arms and cradles me, bringing my lips to his. "I think we should christen this room to celebrate—on the lounger?"

"How about against the wall for a true color match?" I questioned.

"Fuck, baby girl. This is going to be hard and fast." He snarls and grunts, carrying me over to the wall, pinning me with his body as he lifts up my dress, tossing it over my head. "Wow, your tits are spectacular. Soon they're going to be bigger and full of my baby's meal, and mine." His mouth goes straight to my chest, sucking on my flesh. I throw my head back and cry out. They're so tender that every suck goes to my pussy like a nice jolt of pleasure.

My thighs are flexing around his hips, grinding and trying to get my fix.

He's quick to adjust his hips and unleash himself. With a grateful sigh, I moan as he pushes inside me. "So damn tight," he grunts, slamming into me with force, rattling the new hanging frames on the wall.

"If anything breaks, I'll have it repaired, but I'm not stopping until you're screaming my name, Wife."

I cling to him as he violently thrusts into my core, wrecking my heart and soul with his need. Our mouths connect, tasting and kissing in pants and moans. Breathy cries follow every pump, and then I shatter in an intense orgasm. "Damiano," I shout, clawing his back and probably ruining his expensive dress shirt.

"Stella, Stella. Yes, come on my cock. Soak that fucker." He pumps into me, filling me up until there's nothing left, and drops his head on my shoulder with his hands pressed firmly on the painted wall behind him. When I finally catch my breath, I grab his cheeks and lift his head. Those sexy, satiated eyes meet mine and I say, "Yep, it's a perfect match."

EPILOGUE

DAMIANO

It's the heart of summer, and the wife and kids are in the pool while I work in my office. I can almost hear their laughter on the video feed, but it's only a stream, so there's no sound. After a few minutes, I have to turn it off because I'll never finish. With so many damn ventures and operations, legal and illegal, it's hard to focus on it all.

"Thinking about passing the torch?" My father steps into my study as I go over some documents. My brow raises as I eye him. My sons are only seven and three; although they are my twins in almost every way, there's no way they are prepared for the life.

"Funny."

"Frankly, it's just because you've not been as brutal as you used to be." He has a point, but it isn't like he assumed.

"You would have a point if it wasn't for the fact that

my enemies weren't already aware that I'd do anything to protect Stella. Someone comes for her, they won't exist again. I've rebuilt everything that was lost, and destroyed all those that outright opposed me. Is there something I don't know?"

"Nothing. Just curious. Your sister's pregnant again, and I was expecting you to tell me that Stella's pregnant."

"No. I'm starting to think it's part of our lineage. We don't produce many kids."

"It would seem so. I was an only child, and we were blessed with two."

"I'm happy with my small family. If Stella gives me any more babies, I'll be happy, but if not, we have two sons." My boys are growing stronger and smarter every day. We don't need any more kids, even if I wanted a bunch more. It isn't like I don't fuck Stella every single free hour we have, but life is like that. Besides, two boys are enough to handle, especially if they are more like me when they grow up.

"That's good. I'm proud of the man you've become. I never wanted you to live without love, and I'm grateful that Stella was able to open that part of you."

"Thank you, Father. She's the only one who could have."

"I understand. Now, will you be joining us for dinner?"

"Yes. Stella's looking forward to an evening with the family."

"Good, but don't mention the baby news. Gabe and Grace are planning to share the news tonight, and your mother wasn't supposed to tell me."

"For a retired Don, you have very loose lips."

"Some things are worth letting slip," he says, smirking and nodding. I shake my head because my father has gotten soft as hell when it comes to his grandbabies.

A knock interrupts us.

"Enter."

"What is it, Adriano?"

He glances at my father and says, "Mr. Valentino, Sir."

"It's good to see you, Adriano."

I give him a wave of my hand to speak. It's my father, and my business dealings aren't a secret from him. "Boss, there's a problem at the Stokes warehouse. A miscommunication with some of our associates, and they would like a word with you."

"Excuse me, but I have to take care of this."

"I don't have anything to do for a while," my father says.

I smirk—some things just don't run out of the blood. "Care to have some fun?" I ask.

"Don't tell his mother," my father warns Adriano.

"I never saw you, Sir."

"Good." We head out, and my father shows everyone that even retired and sentimental, he's still a fucking killer and unwilling to negotiate. The drive back to the estate was a refreshing one. "Need a change of clothes?"

"No. It's done with, and I don't want her thinking anything other than I was handling business. I'll deal with her wrath when I get home. I just don't want her to worry." As much as my mother would be afraid for his safety, his health would be in danger if there was ever a woman to come between them. She'd cut off his balls. Hell, I'd do it for her. Still, he treasures her more than life itself, which means he won't give her an ounce of jealousy. He'd rather show up covered in blood than make her think he was off having an affair.

"Smart."

I drop him off before returning to my estate and duck into the shower myself. "Last-minute business?" Stella asks, taking my clothes and emptying my pockets, setting everything on the vanity. I love how she just ignores it all, observing me and seeing just me. I can't live without her. My devil needs his angel.

"Yes. Do you want to help wash me off?" I question, giving her a smirk. She drops everything, including the straps to her pretty sundress, letting it fall to the floor. We're totally going to be late to dinner.

Along with that, she was also late...another little Valentino was born nine months later.

ALSO BY CARINA BLAKE

Find out more about Carina Blake:

Website: www.carinablake.com

Facebook: www.facebook.com/AuthorCarinaBlake

Instagram: www.facebook.com/AuthorCarinaBlake

Tiktok: www.tiktok.com/@carinablake

Bookbub: www.bookbub.com/profile/carina-blake

Books:

Bratva Royalty:

Ruthless Kingpin

Bratva Prince

Ruthless Prince

Stolen Hearts Series:

Stolen Wife

Stolen Dove

Stolen Tutor

Stolen Bride

Standalone:

Vegas Baby

www.ingramcontent.com/pod-product-compliance
Lightning Source LLC
Chambersburg PA
CBHW051241250626
47155CB00009B/3119